Praise for Jim Thompson

'If Raymond Chandler, Dashiell Hammett, and Cornell Woolrich could have joined together in some ungodly union and produced a literary offspring, Jim Thompson would be it'

Washington Post

'Jim Thompson is the best suspense writer going, bar none'

New York Times

'Probably the most chilling and believable first-person story of a criminally warped mind I have ever encountered'

Stanley Kubrick

'Jim Thompson's writing is dense, lurid, idiomatic, musical in its speech rhythms . . . plaintive and obscene . . . raucous . . . and bitterly funny'

Village Voice

'The toughest crime novels ever'

Newsweek

'My favourite crime novelist – often imitated but never duplicated – is Jim Thompson'

Stephen King

'A blisteringly imaginative crime novelist . . . he outwrote James M. Cain at his most violent, amoral, terse and fast-moving . . . a classic American writer'

Kirkus Reviews

'A master of the noir crime novel. His vision of small-town America peopled by sophisticated hustlers, dim-witted police officers, corrupt politicians, psychopathic bar-owners and neurotic drunks is uniquely compelling'

Waterstone's Guide to Crime Fiction

Jim Thompson (1906–1977) was born in Anadarko, Oklahoma. Among his many novels are *The Killer Inside Me, The Grifters, Pop. 1280* and *After Dark, My Sweet.* He also wrote two screen-plays (for the Stanley Kubrick films *The Killing* and *Paths of Glory*). *The Getaway* has been filmed twice, in 1972 (by Sam Peckinpah) and in 1994.

By Jim Thompson

Now and On Earth
Heed the Thunder
Nothing More Than Murder
The Killer Inside Me
Cropper's Cabin
Recoil
The Alcoholics
Bad Boy
Savage Night
The Criminal
The Golden Gizmo
Roughneck
A Hell of a Woman
A Swell-Looking Babe
The Nothing Man
After Dark, My Sweet
The Kill-Off
Wild Town
The Getaway
The Transgressors
The Grifters
Pop. 1280
Texas by the Tail
South of Heaven
Ironside (*novelisation*)
The Undefeated (*novelisation*)
Nothing But a Man (*novelisation*)
Child of Rage
King Blood
The Rip-Off

Pop. 1280

Jim Thompson

An Orion paperback

First published in the USA in 1964

This edition published in Great Britain in 2003
by Orion
This paperback edition published in 2006
by Orion Books Ltd,
Orion House, 5 Upper St Martin's Lane,
London WC2H 9EA

An Hachette UK company

5 7 9 10 8 6

Copyright © Jim Thompson 1964

A CIP catalogue record for this book is available
from the British Library.

ISBN 978-0-7528-7961-1

Printed and bound in Great Britain by
Clays Ltd, St Ives plc

The Orion Publishing Group's policy is to use papers that
are natural, renewable and recyclable products and
made from wood grown in sustainable forests. The logging
and manufacturing processes are expected to conform to
the environmental regulations of the country of origin.

www.orionbooks.co.uk

W ell, sir, I should have been sitting pretty, just about as pretty as a man could sit. Here I was, the high sheriff of Potts County, and I was drawing almost two thousand dollars a year – not to mention what I could pick up on the side. On top of that, I had free living quarters on the second floor of the courthouse, just as nice a place as a man could ask for; and it even had a bathroom so that I didn't have to bathe in a washtub or tramp outside to a privy, like most folks in town did. I guess you could say that Kingdom Come was really here as far as I was concerned. I had it made, and it looked like I could go on having it made – being high sheriff of Potts County – as long as I minded my own business and didn't arrest no one unless I just couldn't get out of it and they didn't amount to nothin'.

And yet I was worried. I had so many troubles that I was worried plumb sick.

I'd sit down to a meal of maybe half a dozen pork chops and a few fried eggs and a pan of hot biscuits with grits and gravy, and I couldn't eat it. Not all of it. I'd start worrying about those problems of mine, and the next thing you knew I was getting up from the table with food still left on my plate.

It was the same way with sleeping. You might say I didn't really get no sleep at all. I'd climb in bed, thinking this was one night I was bound to sleep, but I wouldn't. It'd be maybe twenty or thirty minutes before I could doze off. And then, no more than eight or nine hours later, I'd wake up. Wide awake. And I couldn't go back to sleep, frazzled and wore out as I was.

Well, sir, I was layin' awake like that one night, tossing and turning and going plumb out of my mind, until finally I couldn't stand it no longer. So I says to myself, 'Nick,' I says, 'Nick Corey, these problems of yours are driving you plumb out of your mind, so you better think of something fast. You better come to a decision, Nick Corey, or you're gonna wish you had.'

So I thought and I thought, and then I thought some more. And finally I came to a decision.

I decided I didn't know what the heck to do.

I got out of bed that morning, and I shaved and took a bath, even if it was only Monday and I'd washed real good the Saturday before. Then, I put on my Sunday-go-to-meetin' clothes, my new sixty-dollar Stetson and my seventy-dollar Justin boots and my four-dollar Levis. I stood in front of the mirror, checking myself over real good; making sure that I didn't look like some old country boy. Because I was making a little trip to see a friend of mine. I was going to see Ken Lacey and get his advice about my problems. And I always try to look my best when I see Ken Lacey.

I had to pass Myra's bedroom on the way downstairs, and she had her door open to catch the breeze, and without realizing that I was doing it, I stopped and looked in. Then I went in and looked at her some more. And then I eased toward the bed on tippy-toe and stood looking down at her, kind of licking my lips and feeling itchy.

I'll tell you something about me. I'll tell you for true. That's one thing I never had no shortage of. I was hardly out of my shift – just a barefooted kid with my first pair of boughten britches – when the gals started flinging it at me. And the older I got, the more of 'em there were. I'd say to myself sometimes, 'Nick,' I'd say, 'Nick Corey, you'd better do something about these gals. You better start carrying you a switch and whip 'em off of you, or they'll do you to death.' But I never did do nothing like that, because I just never could bear to hurt a gal. A gal cries at me a little, and right away I'm giving in to her.

Well, though, to get back to the subject, I never had no shortage of women and they were all real generous with me. Which maybe don't seem to add up, the way I was staring at my wife, Myra. Licking my lips and feeling itchy all over. Because Myra was quite a bit older than I was and she looked every bit as mean as she was. And believe me, she was one danged mean woman. But the way it is with me, I'm kind of singleminded, I get to thinking about something, and I can't think of anything else. And maybe I wasn't suffering any shortage, but you know how that is. I mean, it's kind of like eating popcorn. The more you have the more you want.

She didn't have a nightdress on, it being summer, and she'd kicked the sheet off. And she was kind of lying on her stomach, so that I couldn't see her face, which made her look a lot better.

So I stood there, staring and steaming and itching, and finally I couldn't stand it no longer and I started unbuttoning my shirt. 'After all, Nick,' I says to myself, 'after all, Nick Corey, this here woman is your wife, and you got certain rights.'

Well, I guess you know what happened. Or I guess you don't know either. Because you don't know Myra, which makes you about as lucky as a person can get. Anyways, she turned over on her back all of a sudden, and opened her eyes.

'And just what,' she said, 'do you think you're doing?'

I told her I was getting ready to take a trip over to the county where Ken Lacey was sheriff. I'd probably be gone until late that night, I said, and we'd probably get real lonesome for each other, so maybe we ought to get together first.

'Huh!' she said, almost spitting the word at me. 'Do you think I'd want you, even if I was of a mind to have relations with a man?'

'Well,' I said. 'I kind of thought maybe you might. I mean, I kind of hoped so. I mean, after all, why not?'

'Because I can hardly stand the sight of you, that's why! Because you're stupid!'

'Well,' I said. 'I ain't sure I can agree with you, Myra. I mean, I ain't saying you're wrong but I ain't saying you're right, either. Anyways, even if I am stupid, you can't hardly fault me for it. They's lots of stupid people in the world.'

'You're not only stupid but you're spineless,' she said. 'You're about the poorest excuse for nothing I ever laid eyes on!'

'Well, looky,' I said. 'If you feel that way, why for did you marry me?'

'Listen to him! Listen to the beast!' she said. 'As if he didn't know why! As if he didn't know that I had to marry him after he raped me!'

Well, that made me kind of sore, you know. She was always saying I'd raped her, and it always made me kind of sore. I couldn't really argue about her saying I was stupid and spineless, because I probably ain't real smart – who wants a smart sheriff? – and I figure it's a lot nicer to turn your back on trouble than it is to look at it. I mean, what the heck, we all got trouble enough of our own without butting in on other people's.

But when she said I was a rapist, *that* was something else. I mean, there just wasn't a word of truth in it. Because it just didn't make sense.

Why for would a fella like me rape a woman, when he had so many generous gals chasing me?

'Well, I'll tell you about this rape business,' I said, getting kind of red in the face as I rebuttoned my shirt. 'I ain't saying you're a liar, because that wouldn't be polite. But I'll tell you this, ma'am. If I loved liars, I'd hug you to death.'

Well, that really started her off. She started blubbering and bawling like a calf in a hail storm. And of course that woke up her half-witted brother, Lennie. So he came rushing in, blubbering and rolling his eyes and slobbering all over his chin.

'What you done to Myra?' he says, spraying spit for about twenty feet. 'What you gone an' done to her, Nick?'

I didn't say anything, being busy dodging the spit. He went stumbling over to Myra, and she took him into her arms, glaring at me.

'You beast! Now look what you've done!'

I said, what the heck, I hadn't done nothing. Far as I could see, Lennie was pretty near always bawling and slobbering. 'About the only time he ain't,' I said, 'is when he's sneaking around town, peeking into some woman's window.'

'You – you bully!' she said. 'Faulting poor Lennie for something he can't help! You know he's as innocent as a lamb!'

I said, 'Yeah, well, maybe.' Because there wasn't much else to say, and it was getting close to train time. I started toward the hall door, and she didn't like that, me walking out without so much as a beg-pardon, so she blazed away at me again.

'You better watch your step, Mr Nick Corey! You know what will happen if you don't!'

I stopped and turned around. 'What will happen?' I said.

'I'll tell the people in this county the truth about you! We'll see how long you'll be sheriff then! After I tell them you raped me!'

'I'll tell you right now what will happen,' I said. 'I'd be run out of my job before I could say scat.'

'You certainly would! You'd better remember it, too!'

'I'll remember,' I said, 'an' here's something for you to remember. If I ain't sheriff, then I got nothing to lose, have I? It don't make a good gosh-damn about anything. And if I ain't sheriff, you ain't the sheriff's wife. So where the heck will that leave you – you and your half-witted brother?'

Her eyes popped and she sucked in her breath with a gasp. It was the first time I'd spoken up to her for a long time, and it kind of took the starch out of her.

I gave her a meaningful nod, and went out the door. When I was about halfway down the stairs, she called to me.

She'd moved real fast, throwing on a robe and working up a smile. 'Nick,' she said, kind of cocking her head to one side, 'why don't you come back for a few minutes, hmmm?'

'I guess not,' I said. 'I'm kind of out of the mood.'

'We-el. Maybe, I could get you back in the mood. Hmmmm?'

I said I guessed not. Anyways, I had to catch a train, and I'd have to grab a bite to eat first.

'Nick,' she said, sort of nervous-like. 'You – you wouldn't do anything foolish, would you? Just because you're angry with me.'

'No, I wouldn't,' I told her. 'No more'n you would, Myra.'

'Well. Have a nice day, dear.'

'The same to you ma'am,' I said. And then I went on downstairs, into the courthouse proper, and out the front door.

I almost took a header as I came out into the dusky haze of early morning. Because the danged place was being painted, and the painters had left their ladders and cans scattered all over everywhere. Out on the sidewalk, I looked back to see what kind of progress they'd been making. The way it looked to me, they hadn't made hardly any at all in the last two, three days – they were still working on the upper front floor – but that wasn't none of my butt-in.

I could have painted the whole building myself in three days. But I wasn't a county commissioner, and I didn't have a painting contractor for a brother-in-law.

Some colored folks had a cook-shack down near the railway station, and I stopped there and ate a plate of corn bread and fried catfish. I was too upset to eat a real meal; too worried about my worries. So I just ate the one plateful, and then I bought another order with a cup of chicory to take on the train with me.

The train came and I got on. I got a seat next to the window, and began to eat. Trying to tell myself that I'd really got Myra told off this morning and that she'd be a lot easier to get along with from now on.

But I knew I was kidding myself.

We'd had showdowns like the one this morning a lot of times. She'd threaten what she was going to do to me, and I'd point out that she had plenty to lose herself. And then things would be a little better for a while – but not really better. Nothing that really mattered was any better.

It wasn't, you see, because it wasn't a fair stand-off between me and her.

She had the edge, and when things came to a showdown, she knew I'd back away.

Sure, she couldn't lose me my job without being a loser herself. She'd have to leave town, her and her low-down half-wit of a brother, and it'd probably be a danged long time before she had it as nice as she had it with me. Probably she'd never have it as nice.

But she *could* get by.

She'd have *something*.

But me . . .

All I'd ever done was sheriffin'. It was all I could do. Which was just another way of saying that all I could do was nothing. And if I wasn't sheriff, I wouldn't have nothing or be nothing.

It was a kind of hard fact to face – that I was just a nothing doing nothing. And that brought up something else for me to worry about. The worry that maybe I could lose my job without Myra saying or doing anything.

Because I'd begun to suspect lately that people weren't quite satisfied with me. That they expected me to do a little something instead of just grinning and joking and looking the other way. And me, I just didn't quite know what to do about it.

The train took a curve and began to follow the river a ways. By craning my neck, I could see the unpainted sheds of the town whorehouse and the two men – pimps – sprawled on the little wharf in front of the place. Those pimps had caused me a sight of trouble, a powerful sight of trouble. Only last week, they'd accidentally-on-purpose bumped me into the river, and a few days before they'd accidentally-on-purpose tripped me up in the mud. And the worst thing of all was the way they talked to me, calling me names and poking mean fun at me, and not showing me no respect at all like you'd naturally expect pimps to show a sheriff, even if he was shaking 'em down for a little money.

Something was going to have to be done about the pimps, I reckoned. Something plumb drastic.

I finished eating and went up to the men's lounge. I washed my hands and face at the sink, nodding to the fella that was sittin' on the long leather bench.

He wore a classy black-and-white checked suit, high-button shoes with spats and a white derby hat. He gave me a long slow look, letting his eyes linger for a moment on my pistol belt and gun. He didn't smile or say anything.

I nodded at the paper he was reading. 'What do you think about them Bullshevicks?' I said. 'You reckon they'll ever overthrow the Czar?'

He grunted, still not saying anything. I sat down on the bench a few feet away from him.

The fact was, I wanted to relieve myself. But I wasn't sure that I ought to go on into the toilet. The door was unlocked swinging back and forth with the motion of the train, and it looked like it must be empty. Still, though, here this fella was, and maybe that's what he was waiting for. So even if the place was empty, it wouldn't be polite to go in ahead of him.

I waited a little while. I waited, squirming and fidgeting, until finally I couldn't wait any longer.

'Excuse me,' I said. 'Were you waiting to go to the toilet?'

He looked startled. Then, he gave me a mean look, and spoke for the first time. 'That's some of your business?'

'Of course not,' I said. 'I just wanted to go to the toilet, and I thought maybe you did, too. I mean, I thought maybe someone was already in there, and that's why you were waiting.'

He glanced at the swinging door of the toilet; swinging wide now so that you could see the stool. He looked back at me, kind of bewildered and disgusted.

'For God's sake!' he said.

'Yes, sir?' I said. 'I don't reckon there's anyone in there, do you?'

I didn't think he was going to answer me for a minute. But then he said, yeah, someone was in the toilet. 'She just went in a little while ago. A naked woman on a spotted pony.'

'Oh,' I said. 'But how come a woman's using the men's toilet?'

'On account of the pony,' he said. 'He had to take a leak, too.'

'I can't see no one from here,' I said. 'It's funny I couldn't see 'em in a little place like that.'

'You calling me a liar?' he said. 'You saying a naked woman on a spotted pony ain't in there?'

I said, no, of course not. I wouldn't say nothing like that. 'But I'm in kind of a hurry.' I said. 'Maybe I better go up to one of the other cars.'

'Oh, no, you don't!' he said. 'No one's calling me a liar and getting away with it!'

'I'm not,' I said. 'I didn't mean it that way at all. I just—'

'I'll show you! I'll show you I'm telling the truth! You're gonna sit right there until that woman and her pony comes out.'

'But I gotta pee!' I said. 'I mean, I really got to, sir.

'Well, you ain't leaving here,' he said. 'Not until you see I'm telling the truth.'

Well, sir, I just didn't know what to do. I just didn't know. Maybe you would have, but I didn't.

All my life, I've been just as friendly and polite as a fella could be. I've always figured that if a fella was nice to everyone, why, they'd be nice to him. But it don't always work out that way. More often than not, it seems like, I wind up in a spot like I was in now. And I just don't know what to do.

Finally, when I was about to let go in my britches, the conductor came through taking up tickets, and I had a chance to get away. I tore out of there in such a hurry that it was maybe a minute before I could get the door open to the next car. And I heard a burst of laughter from the rest room behind me. They were laughing at me, I guess – the conductor and the man in the checked suit. But I'm kind of used to being laughed at, and anyway I didn't have time to think about it right then.

I dashed on up into the next car and relieved myself – and believe me it was a relief. I was coming back down the aisle, looking for a seat in that car so's I wouldn't run into the checked-suit fella again, when I saw Amy Mason.

I was pretty sure that she'd seen me, too, but she let on that she didn't. I hesitated by the seat next to her for a minute, then braced myself and sat down.

No one knows it in Pottsville, because we were careful to keep it a secret, but me and Amy was mighty thick at one time. Fact is, we'd've got married if her Daddy hadn't had such strong objections to me. So we waited, just waiting for the old gentleman to die. And then just a week or so before he did, Myra hooked me.

I hadn't seen Amy since except to pass on the street. I wanted to tell her I was sorry, and try to explain things to her. But she never gave me the chance. Whenever she saw me, she'd toss her head and look away. Or if I tried to stop her, she'd cross to the other side of the street.

'Howdy, Amy,' I said. 'Nice morning.'

Her mouth tightened a little, but she didn't speak.

'It's sure nice running into you like this,' I said 'How far you ridin', if you don't mind my asking?'

She spoke that time. Just barely. 'To Clarkton. I'll be getting ready to leave any moment now.'

'I sure wish you was riding further,' I said. 'I been wanting to talk to you, Amy. I wanted to explain about things.'

'Did you?' She slanted a glance at me. 'The explanation seems obvious to me.'

'Aw, naw, naw,' I said. 'You know I couldn't like no one better'n you, Amy. I never wanted to marry anyone in my life but you, and that's the God's truth. I swear it is. I'd swear it on a stack of Bibles, honey.'

Her eyes were blinking rapidly, like she was blinking back the tears. I got hold of her hand and squeezed it, and I saw her lips tremble.

'Th-then, why, Nick? Why did- y-you—'

'That's what I been wanting to tell you. It's a pretty long story, and – looky, honey, why don't I get off at Clarkton with you, and we can get us a hotel room for a couple hours and—'

It was the wrong thing to say. Right at that time it was the wrong thing.

Amy turned white. She looked at me with ice in her eyes. 'So that's what you think of me!' she said. 'That's all you want – all you ever wanted! Not to marry me, oh, no, I'm not good enough to marry! Just to get me in bed, and—'

'Now, please, honey,' I said. 'I—'

'Don't you dare honey me, Nick Corey!'

'But I wasn't thinking about that – what you think I was thinking about,' I said. 'It was just that it'd take quite a while to explain about me and Myra, and I figured we'd need some place to—'

'Never mind. Just never mind,' she said. 'I'm no longer interested in your explanations.'

'Please, Amy. Just let me—'

'But I'll tell you one thing, Mr Nicholas Corey, and you'd better pass the word along to the proper quarters. If I catch your wife's brother peeking in *my* windows, there's going to be trouble. *Real* trouble. I won't put up with it like the other women in Pottsville do. So you tell her that, and a word to the wise is sufficient.'

I told her I hoped she didn't ever do anything about Lennie. For her own sake, that is. 'I got no more use for Lennie than you have, but Myra—'

'Humph!' She tossed her head and stood up as the train slowed down for Clarkton. 'You think I'm afraid of that – that – her?'

'Well,' I said, 'it might be better if you was. You know how Myra is when she takes out after someone. By the time she gets through gossiping and telling lies, why—'

'Let me out, please.'

She pushed past me and went on up the aisle, her head high, the ostrich plume on her hat dipping and swaying. As the train pulled out, I tried to wave to her where she stood on the platform. But she turned her head quickly, with another swoop of the ostrich plume, and started off up the street.

So that was that, and I told myself that maybe it was just as well. Because how could we ever mean anything to each other the way things stood?

There was Myra, of course, and there was going to be Myra, it looked like, until her or me died of old age. But Myra wasn't the only drawback.

Somehow, I'd gotten real friendly with a married woman, name of Rose Hauck. One of those involvements which I've always kind of drifted into before I knew what was happening. Rose didn't mean a thing to me, except that she was awful pretty and generous. But I meant plenty to her. I meant plenty-plenty, and she'd let me know it.

Just to show how smart Rose was, Myra considered her her very best friend. Yes, sir, Rose could put on that good an act. When we were alone, me and Rose that is, she'd cuss Myra until it actually made me blush. But when they were together, oh, brother! Rose would suck around her – honeyin' and dearie-in' her – until heck wouldn't have it. And Myra would get so pleased and flustered that she'd almost weep for joy.

The surest way of gettin' a rise out of Myra was to hint that Rose was something less than perfect. Even Lennie couldn't do it. He started to one time, just kind of hinted that anyone as pretty as Rose couldn't be as nice as she acted. And Myra slapped him clean across the room.

3

Maybe I didn't tell you, but this Ken Lacey I was going to visit was the sheriff a couple of counties down the river. Me and him met at a peace officers' convention one year, and we kind of cottoned to each other right away. He wasn't only real friendly, but he was plenty smart; I knew it the minute I started talking to him. So the first chance I got, I'd asked him advice about this problem I had.

'Um-hmmm!' he'd said, after I'd explained the situation and he'd thought it over for a while. 'Now, this privy sits on public property, right? It's out in back of the courthouse?'

'That's right,' I said. 'That's exactly right, Ken.'

'But it don't bother no one but you?'

'Right again,' I said. 'You see, the courtroom is on the downstairs rear, and it don't have no windows in back. The windows are up on the second floor where I live.'

Ken asked me if I couldn't get the county commissioners to tear the privy down and I said no, I couldn't hardly do that. After all, a lot of people used it, and it might make 'em mad.

'And you can't get 'em to clean it out?' he asked. 'Maybe sweeten it up a little with a few barrels of lime?'

'Why should they?' I said. 'It don't bother no one but me. I'd probably call down trouble on myself if I ever complained about it.'

'Uh-*hah*!' Ken nodded. 'It'd seem right selfish of you.'

'But I got to do something about it, Ken,' I said. 'It ain't just the hot-weather smell, which is plenty bad by itself, but that's only part of it. Y'see, there's these danged big holes in the roof that show everthing that's going on inside. Say I've got some visitors in, and they think, Oh, my, you must have a wonderful view out that way. So they look out, and the only view they get is of some fella doing his business.'

Ken said, 'Uh-hah!' again, kind of coughing and stroking his mouth. Then, he went on to say that I really had a problem, a *real* problem. 'I can see how it might even upset a high sheriff like you, Nick, with all the pre-occu-pations of your great office.'

'You got to help me, Ken,' I said. 'I'm getting plumb frazzled out of my wits.'

'And I'm *going* to help you,' Ken nodded. 'I ain't never let a brother officer down yet, and I ain't about to begin now.'

So he told me what to do, and I did it. I sneaked out to the privy late that night, and I loosened a nail here and there, and I shifted the floor boards around a bit. The next morning, I was up early, all set to spring into action when the proper time came.

Well, sir, the fella that used the privy most was Mr J. S. Dinwiddie, the bank president. He'd use it on the way home to lunch and on the way back from lunch, and on the way home at night and on the way in in the morning. Well, sometimes he'd pass it up, but never in the morning. By the time he'd got that far from his house his grits and gravy were working on him, and he just couldn't get to the privy fast enough.

He went rushing in that morning, the morning after I'd done my tampering – a big fat fella in a high white collar and a spanking new broadcloth suit. The floor boards went out from under him, and down into the pit. And he went down with them.

Smack down into thirty years' accumulation of night soil.

Naturally, I had him fished out almost as fast as he went in.

So he wasn't really hurt none, just awful messed up. But I never saw one man so mad in all my borned days.

He hopped up and down and sideways, waving his fists and flinging his arms around, and yelling blue murder. I tried to toss some water over him to get the worst of the filth off. But the way he was hopping around and jumping every which way, I couldn't do much good. I'd throw the water at him in one place, and he'd be in another. And cuss! You never heard anything like it, and him a deacon in the church!

The county commissioners came running out, along with the other office holders, all of 'em pretty jittery to see the town's most important citizen like that. Mr Dinwiddie recognized them somehow, although it's hard to see how he could with all that gunk in his eyes. And if he could have found a club, I swear he'd've clubbed 'em.

He cussed 'em up one side and down the other. He swore he'd file felony charges against them for criminal negligence. He yelled that he was going to file personal damage suits against them for wilfully perpetuating a public hazard.

About the only person he had a kind word for was me. He said that a man like me could run the county by himself, and that he was going to see that all the other officials were recalled, because they were just a needless expense and a menace to life and limb as well.

As things turned out, Mr Dinwiddie never did get around to doing anything of the things he threatened to. But that sure settled the privy problem. It was gone and the pit was filled in within an hour; and if you ever feel like getting a punch in the nose, just tell the commissioners that there ought to be another courthouse privy.

Well, that's a sample of Ken Lacey's advice. Just one sample of how good it is . . .

Of course, some people might say it was no good at all, that it might have got Mr Dinwiddie killed and me in a pack of trouble. They might say that the other advice Ken had given me was pure meanness, and meant to be hurtful rather than helpful.

But me, well, I'll always think good of people as long as I possibly can. Or at least I won't think bad about 'em until I absolutely have to. So I hadn't quite reached a decision about Ken as yet.

I figured I'd see how he acted today, what kind of advice he gave me before I made up my mind. If he stacked up even halfway good, I'd give him the benefit of the doubt. But if he didn't appear even that good . . .

Well, I'd know what to do about him.

I always know.

4

I bought a bite of lunch from the train news butch, just a few
sandwiches and some pie and potato chips and peanuts and
cookies and sody-pop. About two o'clock that afternoon, we
got into Ken Lacey's town, the county seat where he was high
sheriff.

It was a real big place – probably four, five thousand people.
The main street was paved, along with the square around the
courthouse, and everywhere you looked there were wire-wheeled
buggies and fancy fringe-topped carriages, and I even seen two,
three auty-mo-biles with eye-goggled dudes driving 'em and
women in veils and linen dusters holding on for dear life. I
mean, it was just like being in New York or one of them other
big cities I've heard about. All that stuff to see, and the people
so busy and used to excitement that they didn't pay no mind at
all.

Just for example, I passed this one vacant lot where there was
the god-dangest dogfight going on that I ever did see. Kind of a
battle royal between two hounds and a bulldog and a kind of
spotty-assed mongrel.

Why, even if there hadn't been a fight, that mongrel would
have been enough to make a fella stop and stare. Because I'm
telling you, he was really something! He had this high ass in the
back, all spotted and speckled like a cow had farted bran on
him. But his front legs were so short that his nose almost rubbed

19

on the ground. And one of his eyes was blue and the other'n was yeller. A real bright yeller like a woman's hair.

I stood there gawking, wishing that I had someone from Pottsville with me as a witness, because naturally no one'd ever believe I'd really seen a dog like that. Then, I happened to look around, and hard as it was to tear myself away, I turned my back on that spectacle and went on toward the courthouse.

I just about had to, you know, unless I wanted people to think I was an old country boy. Because I was the only one that had stopped to look. There was so much going on in that city that no one would ever give a second glance to something like *that*!

Ken and a deputy named Buck, a fella I'd never met before, were sitting in the sheriff's office, slumped way down on their spines with their boots crossed out in front of 'em, and their Stetsons tilted over their eyes.

I coughed and scuffled my feet, and Ken looked up from under his hatbrim. Then he said, 'Why, I'll be god-danged, if it ain't the high sheriff of Potts County!' And he rolled his chair over to me and held out his hand.

'Set down, set down, Nick,' he said, and I sat down in one of the swivel chairs. 'Buck, wake up and meet a friend of mine.'

Buck was already awake, as it turned out, so he rolled over and shook hands like Ken had. Then, Ken kind of jerked his head at him, and Buck rolled over to the desk and got out a quart of white corn and a handful of stogies.

'This here Buck is the smartest deputy I got,' Ken said, as we all had a drink and lit up. 'Got a lot of initiative, Buck has. Don't have to tell him every god-danged thing he's supposed to do like you would some fellas.'

Buck said all he'd ever done was to just try to do his duty, and Ken said, no, sir, he was smart.

'Like old Nick here. That's why he's sheriff of the forty-seventh largest county in this state.'

'Yeah?' Buck said. 'I didn't know they was but forty-seven counties in the state.'

'Pre-zackly!' Ken said, sort of frowning at him. 'How is things in Pottsville these days, Nick? Still booming?'

'Well, no,' I said. 'I wouldn't hardly say that was booming. Pottsville ain't exactly no real metropolis like you got here.'

'Is that a fack?' Ken said. 'Guess my recollection ain't as good as it used to be. Just how big is Pottsville. anyways?'

'Well, sir,' I said, 'there's a road sign just outside of town that says "Pop. 1280," so I guess that's about it. Twelve hundred and eighty souls.'

'Twelve hundred and eighty souls, huh? Is them souls supposed to have people to go with 'em?'

'Well, yeah,' I said, 'that's what I meant. It was just another way of saying twelve hundred and eighty people.'

We all had a couple more drinks, and Buck tossed his stogie in a gaboon and cut himself a chew; and Ken said I wasn't prezackly correct in saying that twelve hundred and eighty souls was the same as twelve hundred and eighty people.

'Ain't that right, Buck?' Ken said, giving him a nod.

'Kee-rect!' Buck said. 'You're a thousand per cent right, Ken!'

'Natcherly! So just tell old Nick why I am.'

'Shorely,' Buck said, turning toward me. 'Y'see it's this way, Nick. That twelve hundred and eighty would be countin' niggers – them Yankee lawmakers force us to count 'em – and niggers ain't got no souls. Right, Ken?'

'Kee-rect!' Ken said.

'Well, now, I don't know about that,' I said. 'I wouldn't come out flat and say you fellas was wrong, but I sure don't reckon I can agree with you neither. I mean, well, just how come you say that colored folks don't have souls?'

'Because they don't, that's why.'

'But why don't they?' I said.

'Tell him, Buck. Make old Nick here see the light,' Ken said.

'Why, shorely,' Buck said. 'Y'see, it's this way, Nick. Niggers ain't got no souls because they ain't really people.'

'They ain't?' I said.

'Why, o' course not. Most everybody knows that.'

'But if they ain't people, what are they?'

'Niggers, just niggers, that's all. That's why folks refer to 'em as niggers instead of people.'

Buck and Ken nodded at me, as if to say there wasn't anything more to be said on this subject. I took another pull at the bottle and passed it around.

'Well, looky here, now,' I said. 'How about this? My mama died almost as soon as I was born, so I was put to suck with a colored mammy. Wouldn't be alive today except for her sucklin' me. Now, if that don't prove—'

'No, it don't,' Ken broke in. 'That don't prove a thing. After all, you could have sucked titty from a cow, but you can't say that cows is people.'

'Well, maybe not,' I said. 'But that ain't the only point of similarity. I've had certain relations with colored gals that I sure wouldn't have with a cow, and—'

'But you could,' Ken said. 'You could. We got a fella over in the jail right now for pleasurin' a pig.'

'Well, I'll be dogged,' I said, because I'd heard of things like that but I never had known of no actual cases. 'What kind of charges you makin' against him?'

Buck said maybe they could charge him with rape. Ken gave him a kind of blank look and said no, they might not be able to make that kind of charge stick.

'After all, he might claim he had the pig's consent, and then where would we be?'

'Aw,' said Buck. 'Aw, now, Ken.'

Ken said, 'What you mean, aw, now. You tryin' to tell me that animals can't understand what you're sayin' to 'em? Why, god-dang it, I got me this little ol' beagle-terrier, and I can say, "Boy, you want to go catch some rats?" and he'll leap all over me, barkin' and whinin' and licking my face. Meaning, natch-erly, that he does want to go after rats. Or I can say, "Boy, you want me to take a stick to you?" an' he'll slink off in a corner with his tail between his legs. Meanin' he don't want me to take a stick to him. An'—'

'Well, sure,' Buck said. 'But—'

'God-dang it!' Ken said. 'Shut up when I'm talking! What the hell's wrong with you, anyways? Here I go an' tell Nick what a smart fella you are, and god-dang if you don't make a liar out of me right in front of him!'

Buck got kind of red in the face, and said he was sure sorry. He sure hadn't meant to contradict Ken. 'I can see just how it happened, now that you explained it to me. This fella, he probably says to the pig, "How about a little you-know-what, Piggie?" and the pig started squealing and twitchin' her tail, meanin' she was ready whenever he was.'

'O' course, that's the way it happened!' Ken scowled. 'So what'd you mean by disputin' me? Why for was you telling me he couldn't have had the pig's consent, and making a god-danged idjit out of yourself in front of a visitin' sheriff? I tell you somethin', Buck,' Ken went on, 'I was entertainin' some pret-ty high hopes for you. Almost had me convinced you was a white man with good sense instead of one of these big-mouth smart-alecks. But now I don't know; I purely don't know. 'Bout all I can say is you shore better watch your step from now on.'

'I shore will. I'm shore sorry, Ken,' Buck said.

'I mean it! I mean every god-danged word of it!' Ken frowned at him. 'You ever go disputin' or contradictin' me again, an' you'll be out in the street scratching horse turds with the sparrows. Or maybe you think you won't be, huh? Maybe you're gonna start arguin' again, tellin' me you won't be out fighting them birds for turds? Answer me, you goddanged liver-lipped idjit!'

Buck sort of choked for a moment, and then he said of course Ken was right. 'You say the word, Ken, an' that's pre-zackly what I'd be doin'.'

'Doin' what? Speak up, god-dang it!'

'S-Scratchin'' – Buck choked again – 'scratchin' horse turds with the sparrers.'

'The hot, steamy kind, right? *Right?*'

'Right,' Buck mumbled. 'You're a thousand per cent right, Ken. I-I reckon there ain't nothin' less appetizin' then a cold horse turd.'

'Well, all right, then,' Ken said, easing up on him and turning to me. 'Nick, I reckon you didn't come all the way up here to hear me an' old stupid Buck jibber-jabberin' at each other. 'Pears to me like you got plenty of troubles of your own.'

'Well, sir, you're sure right about that, Ken,' I said. 'You purely are, an' that's a fact.'

'And you're wantin' my advice, right? You ain't like some smart-alecks that think they already know everthing.'

'Yes, sir,' I said. 'I sure do want your advice, Ken.'

'Uh-hah?' he nodded. 'Uh-hah. Go right ahead, Nick.'

'Well, it's like this,' I said. 'I got this here problem that's been driving me plumb out of my mind. Couldn't hardly sleep nor eat it's been pesterin' me so much. So I fretted and studied an' I thought and I thought, and finally I came to a decision.'

'Uh-huh?'

'I decided I didn't know what to do,' I said.

'Uh-huh,' Ken said. 'Well, now, don't you go rushin' into it. Me an' old Buck here has got plenty on our minds, but we always got time to consult with a friend. Right, Buck?'

'Kee-reck! You're a thousand per cent right, Ken. Like always.'

'So you just take your time an' tell us about it, Nick,' Ken said. 'I'm always willin' to lay aside the cares of my great office when a friend's in trouble.'

I hesitated, wanting to tell him about Myra and her half-wit brother. But all of a sudden, it seemed too personal. I mean, how can you discuss your wife with another fella, even a good friend like Ken was. And what the heck could he do about *her*, even if I did tell him?

So I reckoned I'd better leave her out of it, and take up this other big problem I had. I figured it was one problem he could handle just fine. In fact, now that I'd kind of had a chance to get reacquainted with him, and I'd seen how he handled Buck, I knew he was just the man to take care of it.

5

'Well, sir, Ken,' I said. 'You know that whorehouse there in Pottsville. Place over on the river bank, just a whoop an' a holler from town . . .'

Ken looked up at the ceiling and scratched his head. He allowed that he couldn't say that he did know about it, but he figured naturally that Pottsville had a whorehouse.

'Can't very well run a town without one, right, Buck?'

'Right! Why if they wasn't any whores, the decent ladies wouldn't be safe on the streets.'

'Kee-reck!' Ken nodded. 'Fellas would get all full of piss an' high spirits and take right off after 'em.'

'Well, that's the way I look at it,' I said. 'But now I got this trouble. Y'see, there's these six whores, all nice friendly girls and just as accommodatin' as you could ask for. I really can't make no complaint about these girls. But along with them is these two pimps – one pimp for three girls, I guess – and those pimps are giving me trouble, Ken. They been sassin' me somethin' awful.'

'Now, you don't mean that!' Ken said. 'You don't mean t'tell me that these pimps has actually been sassin' the high sheriff of Potts County!'

'Yes, sir,' I said, 'that's exacly what they've been doin'. An' the bad part about it is, they sometimes done it in front of other people, and a thing like that, Ken, it just don't do a sheriff no good. The word gets around that you've been told off by pimps, and it don't do you no good a'tall!'

'Do tell!' Ken said. 'You spoke the God's truth there, Nick! But I reckon you don't just let 'em get away with it? You taken some action against 'em?'

'Well,' I said, 'I've been sassin' 'em back. I can't say that it's stopped 'em, but I sure been sassin' 'em back, Ken.'

'Sassin' 'em *back*! Why for did you do that?'

'Well, it seemed about right,' I said. 'A fella sasses you, why you just pay him off by sassin' back.'

Ken sort of drew his mouth in, and shook his head. He asked Buck if he'd ever heard such a thing in his life, and Buck said he purely hadn't. Not in all his borned days.

'I'll tell you what you got to do, Nick,' Ken said. 'No, sir, I'll show you what to do. You just stand up and turn your back to me, an' I'll give you an ill-usstrated lesson.'

I did what he told me to. He got up out of his chair, and hauled off and kicked me. He kicked me so hard that I went plumb out the door and half-ways across the hall.

'Now, you come back in here,' he said, crocking a finger at me. 'You just sit down there like you was, so's I can ask you some questions.'

I said I guessed I'd better stand up for a minute, and he said all right, have my own way about it. 'You know why I kicked you, Nick?'

'Well,' I said, 'I guess you probably had a good reason. You were trying to teach me something.'

'Right! So here's what I want to ask you. Say a fella kicks you in the ass like I just did, why what do you do about it?'

'I don't rightly know,' I said. 'No one ever kicked me in the ass before, saving my daddy, God rest his soul, and there wasn't much I could do about it with him.'

'But suppose someone did. Let's just say we got a hypocritical case where someone kicks you in the ass. What would you do about it?'

'Well,' I said. 'I guess I'd kick *him* in the ass. I guess that'd be about right.'

'Turn around,' Ken said. 'You turn right back around again. You ain't learned your lesson yet.'

'Well, looky,' I said. 'Maybe if you could just explain a little more—'

'You turnin' ongrateful?' Ken frowned. 'You tryin' to give orders to a fella when he's trying to help you?'

'No, no, I ain't trying to do that,' I said. 'But—'

'Well, I should hope not! Now, you just turn around like I told you to.'

I turned my back to him again; there just wasn't anything else I could do, it looked like. He and Buck both got up, and they both kicked me at the same time.

They kicked me so hard that I went practically straight up instead of forward. I came down kind of crooked on my left arm, and it hurt so bad that I almost forgot who I was for a moment.

I picked myself up, trying to rub my ass and my arm at the same time. Which just can't be done, in case you're thinking about doing it. I sat down, sore as I was, because I was just too dizzy to stand.

'Hurt your arm?' Ken said. 'Whereabouts?'

'I'm not positive,' I said. 'It could be either the radius or the ulna.'

Buck gave me a sudden sharp look out from under his hatbrim. Sort of like I'd just walked into the room and he was seeing me for the first time. But of course Ken didn't notice anything. Ken had so much on his mind, I reckon, helping poor stupid fellas like me, that he maybe didn't notice a lot of things.

'Now, I guess you learned your lesson, right, Nick?' he said. 'You see the futility of not givin' back no more hurt than what you get?'

'Well, I sure learned some kind of lesson,' I said. 'So if that's the one you was teaching me, I guess that was it.'

'Y'see, maybe the other fella can kick harder'n you can. Or maybe he's got a tougher ass an' it don't hurt him as much as it does you. Or say you got a situation like me an' Buck just demonstrated. Two fellas start kicking you in the ass, so's you get two kicks for every one you give. You get a situation like that, which is just about what you got figuratively speakin', why you could get the ass kicked clean off of you a-fore you had time to tip your hat.'

'But these pimps ain't kicked me,' I said. 'They just been sassin' me, and shovin' me around a little.'

'Same principle. Same principle, pre-zackly. Right, Buck?'

'Right! Y'see, Nick, when a fella starts doin' somethin' bad to you, the proper way to pay him back is t'do somethin' twice as bad to him. Otherwise, the best you got is maybe a stand-off, and you don't never get nothing settled.'

'Kee-reck!' Ken said. 'So I'll tell you what to do about them pimps. The next time they even look like they're goin' to sass you, you just kick 'em in the balls as hard as you can.'

'Huh?' I said. 'But – but don't it hurt awful bad?'

'Pshaw, 'course it don't hurt. Not if you're wearin' a good pair o' boots without no holes in 'em.'

'That's right,' Buck said. 'You just be sure you ain't got any toes stickin' out and it won't hurt you a-tall.'

'I mean, wouldn't it hurt the pimps?' I said. 'Me, I don't think I could stand even an *easy* kick in the balls.'

'Why, shorely, shorely it would hurt 'em,' Ken nodded. 'How else you goin' to make 'em behave if you don't hurt 'em bad?'

'You're actually lettin' 'em off pretty easy, Nick,' Buck said. 'I know I'd sure hate to be in the same room if any pimp sassed old Ken here. Ken wouldn't stop with just kickin' 'em. Why, a-fore they knew what was happening, he'd just yank out his pissoliver and shoot 'em right in their sassy mouths.'

'Pre-zackly!' Ken said. 'I'd send them sassy skunks to hell without no fooling around about it.'

'So you're really being too easy on 'em, Nick. A god-danged

sight easier than a proud, intelligent upstandin' officer like ol' Ken. Ken would shoot 'em deader'n doornails, if he was in your place, and you heard him say so yourself.'

'Right!' said Ken. 'I sure wouldn't miss doing pre-zackly that.'

Well . . .

It looked like I'd got what I came for, and it was getting kind of late by then. So I thanked Ken for his advice, and stood up. I was still just a little wobbly, though; kind of rocking on my heels. And Ken asked me if I was sure I could make it to the station all right.

'Well, I guess so,' I said. 'I sure hope so, anyways. It sure wouldn't seem right for me to ask you to walk me there after everything you've already done for me.'

'Why, you don't need to ask!' Ken said. 'You think I'd let you go all the way to the train alone, a fella that looks as peaked as you do?'

'Well, I wouldn't want to trouble you none,' I said.

'Trouble?' Ken said. 'Why, it's a positive pleasure! Buck, you just heist yourself up out of that chair, and walk Nick to the depot.'

Buck nodded and heisted himself up. I said I sure hoped I wasn't putting him to any bother, and he said it wouldn't be no bother a-tall.

'Just so's you can bear with me,' he said. 'Know I can't be no ways as good a comp'ny for you as a fella like Ken.'

'Well, now, I'm sure you'll be just fine,' I said. 'Bet you'll prove out a real interestin' fella.'

'I'll try,' Buck promised. 'Yes, sir, I'll purely try, and that's a fack.'

6

had supper down near the depot, buying a whopping big meal for Buck along with my own. Then, my train came and Buck walked me down to the car I was riding in. Not that I couldn't have made it all right by myself – I was feeling pretty good about then. But we were getting along real fine, just like I thought we might, and we had a lot of things to say to each other.

I fell asleep almost as soon as I'd given my ticket to the conductor. But I didn't sleep good. Dog-tired as I was, I drifted into a scary dream, the nightmare that was always a-haunting me. I dreamed that I was a kid again only it didn't seem like a dream. I *was* a kid living in the old rundown plantation house with my daddy. Trying to keep out of his way, and never being able to. Getting beat half to death every time he could grab me.

I dreamed I was ducking into a doorway, thinking I'd got away from him. And suddenly being grabbed from behind.

I dreamed I was putting his breakfast on the table. And trying to get my arms up when he flung it in my face.

I dreamed – I *lived* – showing him the reading prize I'd won in school. Because I was sure that would please him, and I just had to show it to someone. And I dreamed – *lived* – picking myself up off the floor with my nose bloodied from the little silver cup. And he was yelling at me, shouting that I was through with school because I'd just proved I was a cheat along with everything else.

The fact was, I guess, that he just couldn't stand for me to be any good. If I was any good, then I couldn't be the low-down monster that had killed my own mother in getting born. And I had to be that. He had to have someone to blame.

I don't fault him much for it any more, because I've seen a lot of people pretty much like he was. People looking for easy answers to big problems. People that blame the Jews or the colored folks for all the bad things that happen to 'em. People that can't realize that a heck of a lot of things are bound to go wrong in a world as big as this one. And if there is any answer to why it's that way – and there ain't always – why, it's probably not just one answer by itself, but thousands of answers.

But that's the way my daddy was – like those people. They buy some book by a fella that don't know a god-dang thing more than they do (or he wouldn't be having to write books). And that's supposed to set 'em straight about everything. Or they buy themselves a bottle of pills. Or they say the whole trouble is with other folks, and the only thing to do is to get rid of 'em. Or they claim we got to war with another country. Or . . . or God knows what all.

Anyway, that's how my daddy was. That's the way I grew up. It's no wonder, I reckon, that me and the girls always got along so well. I reckon I really worked at getting along with 'em; sort of made a trade out of it without really knowing I was doing it. Because a fella has to have someone that likes him. He just naturally has to. And girls are just naturally inclined to like a man.

I guess when you come right down to it, I was making the same mistake that those people I was talking about make. Because there ain't no bigger problem than love, nothing is truly hard to come by, and I was looking for an easy answer to it.

7

Well, sir, danged if I hadn't got back to Pottsville on just about the darkest night of the year. It was so dark that I could have had a firefly sitting on my nose and I wouldn't have been able to see it.

Of course, the dark didn't really bother me. The way I knew every nook and cranny of Pottsville, I could get to wherever I wanted to go if I was walking in my sleep. So the dark was really an advantage to me, rather than otherwise. If anyone was up and around, and of course there wouldn't be at that time of night, they wouldn't see where I was going and wonder why I was going there.

I walked right down the dark middle of Main Street. I turned south at the end of it, and headed toward the river. There was just a speck of light down that way, sort of a little blob bulging up out of the darkness. I figured it came from the whorehouse, or rather from the little pier behind it. Those two pimps would be sitting out there, I knew, taking the night air and drinking themselves stiff.

They'd be feeling their oats for sure by the time I got there. All sassy and nasty, and primed for meanness toward a fella that'd always been nice to them.

I struck a match, took a quick look at my watch, I began to walk faster. The steamer, *Ruby Clark*, was about due and I had to be on hand when it rounded the bend.

There'd been a pretty hard rain the week before; low river country, there's always a lot of rain. The wet was all dried up by now, because we get a lot of hot sunshine too. But the road had gotten rutted here and there, and hurrying like I was I brought my foot down where I shouldn't have.

I stumbled, almost taking a header before I could right myself. I paused, sort of getting my breath back, and then I whirled around. Straining my eyes and ears, scared stiff for a minute. Because I'd heard something. The same kind of clod-kicking sound I'd made, only not so loud.

I held my breath, telling myself that there couldn't be anyone following me. Knowing that even if there was someone back there, I was still protected by the darkness.

I stood stock still for two, three minutes. Then, I heard the sound again and I recognized it for what it was, and I almost laughed out loud with relief.

It was just some of those god-danged big nightbeetles we have down here. They go swooping around, looking for each other, and then they come together in mid-air and go plunking down on the ground.

They can make a heck of a racket on a stilly night. If you're maybe just a little uneasy like I was, they can give you a bad start.

It was two or three minutes later when I got to the whore-house. I tippy-toed along the walk which ran down the side of the place, and went around to the rear.

The two pimps were there, right where I thought they'd be. They were sitting down with their backs to the mooring posts, a dimmed lantern and a jug of whiskey between them. They looked at me owl-eyed as I came in out of the darkness, and then the one named Curly, a kind of dude-ish fella with kinky scalp-tight hair, shook a finger at me.

'Now, Nick, you know you're not supposed to come over here but once a week. Just once a week, and only long enough to pick up your graft and get.'

'That's right,' said the one named Moose. 'Fact is, we're bein' mighty generous to let you come here at all. We got a reputation to protect here, and it sure doesn't help none to have a fella like you dropping around.'

'Well, now,' I said, 'that's not a very nice thing to say.'

'Oh, well, there's nothing personal in it,' Curly said. 'It's just one of those unpleasant facts of life. You're a crook, and it doesn't look good to have crooks around.'

I asked him how come he thought I was a crook, and he said what else could I call myself. 'You take graft, don't you? You're getting a dollar out of every five that comes in here?'

'But I have to,' I said. 'I mean, it's kind of a civic duty. If I didn't keep you people stripped down a little, you'd get too powerful. First thing I know, you'd be running the county instead of me.'

Moose sneered and wobbled to his feet. 'You two-bit clown,' he said, 'will you just get the hell out of here? Will you, or am I gonna have to make you?'

'Well, now,' I said. 'Well, now, I don't know about that. I figure that's a pretty mean way to talk to a fella that's always been nice to you.'

'Are you gonna get or not?' He took a step toward me.

'You'd better, Nick,' Curly nodded, pushing himself up. 'You kind of make us sick to our stomachs, you know? It may not be your fault, but the air turns bad every time you show up.'

Around the bend, I could see the lights of the *Ruby Clark*, and I could hear the whip of the paddles as it fought for the turn. It was that time, it would be that time any second now, and I upholstered my gun and took aim.

'Wha—!' Moose stopped dead in his tracks, his mouth gaping open.

Curly said, 'Oh, now, Nick!' forcing a smile to his face. But it was the sickest smile I'll ever see.

That's one thing people always know, I guess. They know

when they're going to die. And Moose and Curly knew that they were going to.

'Good night, ye merry gentlemen,' I said. 'Hail and farewell.'

The *Ruby Clark* whistled.

By the time the echo died, Moose and Curly were in the river, each with a bullet spang between his eyes.

I waited on the little pier for a minute until the *Ruby* had gone by. I always say there's nothing prettier than a steamboat at night. Then I went around on the catwalk, and headed for home.

The courthouse was dark, naturally, when I got there. I took off my boots and crept up the stairs. And I got in bed without waking anyone.

I fell asleep right away. A couple of hours later I waked up, with Myra shaking me.

'Nick! *Nick!* Will you please get up, for pity's sake!'

'Huh! What?' I said. 'What's going on, Myra?'

But I heard it then, the pounding on the downstairs door. A fella would've had to be deaf not to hear it.

'Well, I'll be dogged,' I said. 'Now, who in tarnation can that be?'

'Well, go and see, darn it! Get down there before they wake poor Lennie up!'

I studied about it for a moment, staying right where I was while Myra went on nagging at me. Then I said I wasn't sure whether I should go downstairs or not, because why for would any honest person be pounding on doors at this time of night?

'It might be robbers, Myra,' I pointed out. 'Wouldn't be a bit surprised if that's who it was. I hear they do their robbin' late at night when decent folks is in bed.'

'You fool! You stupid, spineless, cowardly slob! Are you the sheriff of this county or not?' Myra yelled.

'Well,' I said, 'I guess you could say that.'

'And isn't it the sheriff's job to take care of criminals? Isn't it? Answer me, you – you—!'

'Well, I guess you could say that, too,' I said. 'I ain't thought much about it, but it sounds reasonable.'

'You – you get down there!' Myra spluttered. 'Doggone you, you get right down there this minute, or I'll – I'll—'

'But I ain't got no clothes on,' I said. 'Nothin' but my long-handled drawers. Wouldn't hardly seem right goin' to the door without no clothes on.'

Myra's voice dropped so low that I could hardly hear it, but her eyes flashed fire. 'Nick,' she said, 'this is the last time I'm going to tell you. You go to the door right this minute, or you'll wish you had! You'll really wish you had!'

The pounding was getting a lot louder by now, and someone was shouting my name, someone that sounded an awful lot like Ken Lacey. So, what with Myra carrying on like she was, I figured maybe I'd better go to the door.

I swung my legs over the side of the bed, and pulled on my boots. I studied 'em a minute, wetting my finger with spit and rubbing down a little scuffed place. I yawned and stretched, and scratched under my armpits.

Myra let out a groan. She snatched up my britches and flung 'em at me, so that the legs wrapped around my neck like a scarf.

'You ain't mad about somethin', are you honey?' I said, getting the britches untangled and starting to draw 'em on. 'I sure hope I ain't annoyed you no way.'

She didn't say anything. Just started to swell up like she was about to explode.

'I got a trade-last for you,' I said. 'A fella was saying to me the other day, he said, "Nick, you got the prettiest mother in town." So I asked him who he meant, naturally, because my mama's been dead for years. And he said, "Why, that lady you call Myra. You mean to tell me she ain't your mother?" That's just what he said, honey. So now you got to tell me something nice that someone said about me.'

She still didn't say anything. She just leaped at me, sort of meowing like a cat, her hands clawed to scratch my eyes out.

She didn't do it, because I'd been kind of expecting something like that. All the time I was talking to her, I was easing back toward the door. So instead of landing on me, she came up against the wall, clawing the heck out of it a-fore she could come to her senses.

Meantime, I went on downstairs and opened the door.

Ken Lacey busted in. He was wild-eyed, heaving for breath. He grabbed me by the shoulders and started shaking me.

'Have you done it yet?' he said. 'God-dang it, have you already gone an' done it?'

'Wh-what?' I tried to shake free of him. 'Have I gone an' done what?'

'You know what, god-dang it! What I told you to do! Now, you answer me, you consarned idjit, or I'll beat it out of you!'

Well, sir, it looked to me like he was pretty excited about something. Might get himself in such a tizzy that he'd keel over with the frantics. So I just pushed him into my office and made him set down at my desk, and I struck a lamp and made him take a big drink of whiskey. And then, when he seemed to be calmed down a little, I asked him just what it was all about.

'What am I supposed to have done, Ken? The way you're actin', you'd think I'd killed someone.'

'Then you didn't,' he said, his eyes hard on my face. 'You didn't kill anyone.'

'Kill anyone?' I said. 'Why, what a riddicerlous question! Why for would I kill anyone?'

'And you didn't? You didn't kill them two pimps that was sassing you?'

'Ken,' I said. 'How many times have I got to tell you? Why for would I kill anyone?'

He heaved a big sigh, and relaxed for the first time. Then, after another long drink, he slammed down the jug and began to cuss his deputy, Buck.

'God-dang, just wait until I get hold of him! Just you wait!

I'll kick his mangy ass s'hard he'll have to take off his boots to comb his hair!'

'Why, what'd he do?' I said. 'What's old Buck gone an' done?'

'He frazzled me, that's what! Got me so god-danged excited an' worried that I was plumb out of my mind,' Ken said, cussing Buck up one side and down the other. 'Well, it's my own god-danged fault, I reckon. Had the proof right before me that he was a low-down maniac, but broad-minded like I am, I went and closed my eyes to it.'

'How come?' I said. 'What you mean you had the proof, Ken?'

'I mean I caught him reading a book, that's what! Yes, sir, I caught him red-handed. Oh, he claimed he was only lookin' at the pitchers, but I knew he was lyin'.'

'Well, I'll be dogged!' I said. 'I will be double-dogged! But what's Buck got to do with you being down here?'

So Ken told me how it had happened.

It seemed like after he left me, Buck went back to the office and began to fret out loud. Wonderin' whether I'd really be crazy enough to kill those pimps, which would leave Ken in a peck of trouble. The way Buck saw it – in his out-loud worryin' – Ken had told me I should kill 'em, and if I went ahead and did it he'd be just as guilty as I was.

He kept on fretting about it, Buck did, saying I just *might* kill the pimps because I'd always taken Ken's advice in the past, no matter how nutty it was. And then when he saw how upset Ken was getting, he said that the law probably wouldn't be too hard on him. Probably wouldn't be hard on him, a-tall, like they would me, but maybe let him off with thirty, forty years.

The upshot of it was that Ken finally tore out of his office, and caught the Red Ball freight to Pottsville. He hadn't had too nice a trip because the caboose, where he was sittin' had had an awful flat wheel. He said he was probably a lot sorer in the behind than I was from getting kicked, and all he wanted to do now was go to bed.

'I just had more'n one poor body can stand in a day,' he yawned. 'I reckon you can put me up all right, can't you?'

I said that I was right shamed, but no, I couldn't. We just didn't have no place where an extra fella could be bedded down.

'God-dang it!' he scowled. 'All right, I'll go to the hotel, then!'

I allowed that that might be kind of hard to do, seeing that Pottsville didn't have a hotel. 'If it was daytime, you could bed at the Widder Shoup's place; that's what the travellin' salesmen do. But she sure wouldn't let you in at this time of night.'

'Well, where the god-danged hell am I gonna sleep, then?' he said, 'I sure as heck ain't sittin' up all night!'

'Well, let's see now,' I said. 'Danged if I can only think of but one place, Ken. A place that could bed you down. But I'm afraid you wouldn't get much sleep there.'

'You just lead me to it! I'll do the sleepin'!'

'Not at the whorehouse you wouldn't,' I said. 'Y'see, the girls ain't had much business lately, and they'd all be mighty raunchy. Prob'ly be makin' demands on you all night long.'

'Uh-hah!' Ken said. 'Well, now! I reckon a fella can put up with anything if he has to. Nice young gals, are they!'

'No, they ain't,' I said. 'Most of 'em are fairly young, maybe seventeen, eighteen. But they got this one old gal that's every bit of twenty-one. And she just won't leave a fella alone! She purely won't, Ken, and it wouldn't be fair not to warn you.'

A streak of spit was trickling down his chin. He brushed it away and stood up, a kind of glassy look in his eyes.

'I better be goin',' he said. 'I better be goin' right this minute.'

'I'll put you on the right road,' I said. 'But there's something you got to know first. About them two pimps . . .'.

'Don't you worry none. I'll take care of 'em!'

'You won't have to,' I said, 'because they won't be there.

They'll be off somewheres drunk by now, and they won't wake up until noon.'

'What the hell, then?' Ken took a fidgety step toward the door. 'If the girls think they ain't there—'

'But they *don't* think that. The pimps have got 'em kidded that they're watching the place day and night, which naturally makes it hard for the girls to relax and have fun like they want to. So—'

'Uh-huh? Yeah, yeah,' Ken said. 'Go on, god-dang it.'

'So here's what you do as soon as you go in. You tell the girls that you've taken care of the pimps real good, and that they won't be nosing around a-tall. You tell 'em that, and everything will be just fine an' dandy.'

He said he'd tell 'em what I said to. (And as it turned out, he told them exactly that.) Then, he went out the door and across the yard, moving so fast that I could hardly keep up with him.

We crossed through the edge of town, and I lined him up on the river road. He went on by himself, then, without so much as a nod. And then I reckon he remembered his manners, because he turned around and came back.

'Nick,' he said, 'I'm obliged to you. Maybe I ain't been too nice to you in the past, but I ain't forgettin' what you've done here tonight!'

'Aw, pshaw,' I said. 'Comes to that, Ken, I ain't forgetting all the things you've done, neither.'

'Well, anyways, I'm obliged to you,' he said.

'Why, it was a positive pleasure doin' it,' I said. 'A positive pleasure, and that's a fact.'

8

Ken showed up at breakfast time the next morning, looking mighty peaked and pale and wrung-out. But all shook-up as he was, he managed to toss a lot of flattery at Myra and to say a few kind words to Lennie, so she treated him pretty nice. Not real nice, because she knew he'd spent the night in the whorehouse – which was the only place he could have spent it – but as nice as a lady could treat a gentleman under the circumstances. She kept urging him to have something to eat, and Ken kept turning it down with thanks and saying that he hardly ever et anything in the morning but just a little coffee, which was all he wanted now.

'I got to watch my weight, ma'am,' he said. 'I ain't got a naturally handsome figure like you and your fine-looking brother.'

Lennie giggled and spit at him; feelin' pleased, you know. Myra blushed and said he was just a great big flatterer.

'Me? Me, flatter a woman?' Ken said. 'Why, I never heard the like!'

'Oh, you! You know I don't have a *really* good figure.'

'Well, maybe not. But that's because you ain't fully developed yet,' Ken said. 'You're still a young girl.'

'Tee-hee,' Myra giggled. 'You awful thing, you!'

'You just wait until you fill out a little,' Ken said. 'Wait until you're as old as your brother.'

Well, sir, lies like that can take a lot out of a man even when he's feeling good. Which Ken sure wasn't. He was just carrying on out of habit, and from the looks of him he was just about to the end of his rope. Fortunately, it seemed to occur to Myra about then that she was being a little too friendly with Ken and that she was letting him get pretty gay with her. So she froze up all of a sudden, and started clearing away the dishes. And Ken said his thank-yous and goodbyes, and I got him downstairs to my office.

I handed him a quart bottle of white whiskey. He took a long, long drink, gagged, gulped and leaned back in his chair. Sweat popped out on his forehead. He shuddered all over, and his face turned a few shades whiter. For a minute I thought he was going to be one sick man; all that lying and flattering to Myra had been just too much for him. Then, all at once, the color flooded back into his face, and he stopped sweating and shaking. And he drew a long, deep sigh.

'God-dang!' he said softly. 'I shore needed that.'

'Fella can't ride a horse with one stirrup,' I said. 'Have another one, Ken.'

'Well, god-dang it,' he said. 'God-dang it, Nick, I don't care if I do.'

He had a couple more drinks, which brought the bottle down to about the halfway level. Then he said he guessed he'd better slow down a little bit. And I told him to just take his time, he couldn't get a train back home for a couple of hours yet.

We sat there for a minute or two, not saying much of anything. He looked at me and looked away again, and a kind of shy-sly look came over his face.

'Mighty handsome young fella your brother-in-law,' he said. 'Yes, sir, mighty handsome.'

'And he's an idjit,' I said. 'Anyways, he sure ain't quite right in the head.'

Ken nodded and said, yeah, he'd noticed that. 'But maybe

that might not make too much difference to a certain kind of woman, you know, Nick? Say a woman that was a lot older than he was. A woman that was pretty ugly and pretty apt to stay that way.'

'Well, I just don't know about that,' I said. 'I wouldn't say you were wrong but I sure wouldn't say you was right either.'

'Well, maybe that's because you ain't real bright,' Ken said. 'Why, I'll bet you there's a woman right in this town that would really *pree-fer* Lennie to a fella like you. I ain't saying that you ain't a plenty good-lookin' fella yourself, but probably you ain't got as long a dingle-dangle as he has – they tell me them idjits are hung like a stud-hoss. And, anyways—'

'Well, now, I don't know about that,' I said. 'I ain't never had any complaints in that department yet.'

'Shut up when I'm talkin'!' Ken said. 'Shut up and maybe you'll learn somethin'! I was about to say that everything else being equal, which I doubt like hell in your case because all of them idjits have got dongs you could skip rope with, *but* – but irregardless of that a woman still might rather have a dummy pour it on her than a normal fella. Because she don't have to put on for him, know what I mean? She can boss him around. She can be just as haggy as all hell and twice as mean, and she can still get what she needs.'

I scratched my head and said, well, maybe so. But I still thought he was wrong about Lennie. 'I know for a fact that there ain't no woman in this town that's got any use for him. They pretend that they do, to keep on the good side of Myra, but I know they all hate his guts.'

'*All* of 'em!'

'All of 'em. Except Myra, of course. His sister.'

Ken snorted and ran his hand over his mouth. Then, he kind of got a grip on himself, and his talk slowed down a little. But he still couldn't get off the subject.

'Ain't much family resemblance between Lennie and your

wife. Hardly know they was brother an' sister unless someone told you.'

'That's right, I guess,' I said. 'Can't say that I ever thought much about it.'

But I had thought about it. Yessir, I'd thought plenty about it.

'Was you acquainted with Lennie before you married? Know that you was goin' to have a idjit for a brother-in-law?'

'Well, no, I didn't,' I said. 'I didn't even know that Myra had a brother until afterwards. Came as quite a surprise for me.'

'Uh-hah!' Ken snorted. 'Well, don't be surprised if you get another surprise some time, Nick. No, sir, don't you be surprised at all.'

'What?' I said. 'How do you mean, Ken?'

He shook his head, not answering me, and broke out laughing. I laughed right along with him.

Because it was a pretty good joke, you see. *I* was a joke. And maybe I couldn't do anything about it right now, but I figured I would some day.

Ken took a couple more long drinks. I stood up and said maybe we'd better be going. 'Got quite a little walk to the station, and I want you to meet a few fellas. Be a big treat for 'em to meet a big-city sheriff like you.'

'Why, now, I bet it would be that,' Ken said, staggering to his feet. 'Prob'ly ain't every day they get to meet a real man in a pisspot of a town like this.'

'Tell 'em how you took care of them two pimps,' I said. 'They'll be right impressed hearin' how you took on two pimps all by yourself, and gave 'em what-for.'

He blinked at me owlishly. He said, what pimps, what the god-danged hell was I talking about, anyway? I said, the pimps I'd warned him about last night – the two that were bound to try to give him some trouble.

'Huh?' he said. 'What? Did you tell me somethin' like that?'

'You mean you let 'em get away with it?' I said. 'Ken Lacey took dirt from a couple of low-down pimps?'

'Hah? What?' He rubbed his hand over his eyes. 'Who says I took dirt from pimps?'

'I knew you didn't!' I said, giving him a slap on the back. 'Not Ken Lacey, the bravest, smartest peace officer in the state.'

'Well,' said Ken. 'Uh, you shorely spoke a mouthful there, Nick. You shorely did, and that's a fact!'

'Any other man, I wouldn't have let him go over there last night. But I knew you could stand up to those pimps if they come at you with guns and knives. I knew you'd make 'em wish they'd never been born.'

Ken put a stern look on his face, like that fella William S. Hart does in the movies. He squared his shoulders and straightened up, or as much as he could straighten with the whiskey wobbling his legs.

'What'd you do to 'em, Ken?' I said. 'How did you settle their hash, anyways?'

'I, uh, I took care of 'em, that's what.' He gave me a lopsided wink. 'You know, I – *hic*! – took care of 'em.'

'Good. You took care of 'em for good, Ken?'

'God-danged right, I did. Them's two pimps that won't never bother a white man no more!'

He started looking around for the whiskey bottle. I pointed out that he was holding onto it, so he had himself a couple more drinks, and then he held the bottle up to the light.

'Why, god-dang! Danged if I ain't drunk almost a whole quart of whiskey!'

'What the heck?' I said. 'It don't hardly show on you none.' And the funny part of it was that it suddenly didn't show much.

I'd seen him drink before, and I knew how whiskey acted on him. A fairly small amount of booze, say, a pint or so, and he'd get drunk as a skunk. He'd show it, I mean. But when he went over that certain amount – and up to a point, of course – he'd seem to sober up. He'd stop staggering, stop slurring his words, stop playing the fool in general. Inside, he'd still be dead drunk, but you'd never know it by looking at him.

He finished the rest of the whiskey, and we headed for the railroad station. I introduced him to everyone we met, which was a big part of the population, and he stuck out his chest and told everyone how he'd taken care of the two pimps. Or rather, he just said that he *had* taken care of 'em.

'Never mind how,' he'd say. 'Never you mind how.' And then he'd wink and nod, and everybody would be pretty impressed.

We stopped to talk to so many people that it was only a couple of minutes before train time when we got to the station. I shook hands with him and then, before I realized I was doing it, I laughed out loud.

He gave me a suspicious look; asked me what I was laughing about.

'Nothing much,' I said. 'I was just thinkin' how funny it was you rushing down here last night. Thinkin' I might kill those pimps.'

'Yeah,' he grinned sourly, 'that is funny. Imagine a fella like you killing anyone."

'You can't imagine me doing it, can you, Ken? You just can't, can you?'

He said he sure couldn't, and that was a fact. 'If I'd stopped to think, instead of letting that god-danged Buck get me all riled up—'

'But it would be easy to imagine you doing that killing, wouldn't it, Ken? Killing wouldn't bother you a bit.'

'What?' he said. 'What do you mean, I—'

'In fact, folks wouldn't have to do any imagining, would they? You've as good as admitted it to dozens of people.'

He blinked at me. Then the wild sweat broke out on his face again, and a streak of spit oozed from the corner of his mouth. And there was fear in his eyes.

It had soaked in on him at last, the spot he was in. Soaked clear through a quart of booze until it hit him where he lived and rubbed the place raw.

'Why – why, god-dang you!' he said. 'I was just makin' talk! You know danged well I was! I never even seen those pimps last night!'

'No, sir, I bet you didn't.' I grinned at him. 'I'd bet a million dollars you didn't.'

'Y-you—' He gulped. 'You m-mean you did k-kill—'

'I mean, I know you're a truthful man,' I said. 'If you said you didn't see those pimps, I know you *didn't* see 'em. But other folks might think somethin' else, mightn't they, Ken? If those pimps' bodies was to crop up some place, everybody'd think that you killed them. Couldn't hardly think nothin' else under the circumstances.'

He cussed and made a grab at me. I stayed where I was, grinning at him, and he slowly let his hands drop to his side.

'That's right, Ken,' I nodded. 'That's right. There ain't a thing you can do but hope. Just hope that if someone *did* kill those pimps that no one ever finds their bodies.'

The train was coming in.

I waited until it came to a stop; and then, since Ken seemed too dazed to do it by himself, I helped him on.

'One other thing, Ken,' I said, and he turned on the step to look at me. 'I'd be real nice to Buck, if I was you. I got kind of a funny idea that he don't like you very much as it is, so I sure wouldn't do no more talkin' about makin' him peck horse turds with the sparrers.'

He turned back around again, and went on up the steps.

I started back through town.

9

I'd been thinking it was about time to do some political campaignin', since I had a pretty tough opponent coming up for a change. But I figured there'd been enough going on for one morning, what with Ken's big talk; and anyways, I just didn't have a campaign plan this time.

Always before, I'd let the word get around that I was against this and that, things like cockfighting and gambling and whiskey and so on. So my opposition would figure they'd better come out against 'em, too, only twice as strong as I did. And I went right ahead and let 'em. Me, almost anyone can make a better speech than I can, and anyone can come out stronger against or for something. Because, me, I've got no very strong convictions about anything. Not any more I haven't.

Well, anyway, by the time it got ready to vote, it looked like a fella wouldn't be able to have no fun at all any more, if my opponents were elected. About all a fella would be able to do, without getting arrested, was to drink sody-pop and maybe kiss his wife. And no one liked the idea very much, the wives included.

So, all and all, I began to look pretty good to folks. It was a case of nothing looking better than something, because all anyone had to do was listen to me and look at me a while to know that I wasn't against anything very much, except having my pay stopped, and that I wouldn't have enough gumption to do anything even if I did want to. I'd just let things go along like they always had, because there wasn't much point in trying to change 'em. And when the votes were counted, I was still sheriff.

I'm not saying that there weren't a lot of folks who really liked me. There *was* a lot of 'em, folks that I'd been kids with and who knew me as a nice friendly fella who was always ready to do a favor if it didn't put him out of pocket too much or offend someone else. But it seemed to me that I didn't have as many friends as I'd used to. Even the very folks I'd favored, them most of all, it seemed like, weren't as friendly as they had been. They seemed to kind of hold it against me because I *hadn't* cracked down on 'em. And I didn't know quite what to do about it, since I'd never really got the habit of doing anything, and I didn't know how I was going to get myself elected again. But I knew I was going to have to do *something*. I was going to have to do something or think of something entirely different from the stuff I'd come up with in the past. Or I'd be out of a job when fall came.

I rounded the corner from the depot, and turned into Main Street. Then I started to duck back off of it, because there was a heck of a racket a couple of blocks down the street, a lot of fellas jamming the sidewalk. It looked like a fight of some kind was going on, which meant that I'd better get out of sight before I had to arrest someone besides maybe getting hurt myself.

I started to dart back around the corner; then, somehow, I caught myself, and I went on down the street to where the ruckus was.

It wasn't really a fight, like I'd been afraid of. Just Tom Hauck beating a colored fella named Uncle John. It seemed like Tom had been coming out of the hardware store with a box of shotgun shells when Uncle John had bumped into him or vice versa. Anyway, he'd dropped the shells and some of 'em had spilled off into the street mud. Which was why he'd grabbed hold of the colored fella and started beating him.

I pushed myself between them, and told Tom to stop.

I felt kind of funny about it, because Tom was the husband of Rose Hauck, the gal who was so generous with me. I guess a fella always feels kind of funny in a situation like that; guilty, I mean, like he ought to give the fella any break that he can. Aside from that, Tom was a lot bigger than I was – mean fellas are always bigger than I am – and he was about half-loaded with booze.

About all Tom ever did was booze-up and go hunting. His wife, Rose, did most of the farm work when she wasn't laid up from Tom beating her. Tom would set her chores for her, before he went off on a hunting trip. They were usually more than a strong man and a boy could do, but if Rose didn't have 'em done by the time he got back, she was in for a beating.

Now, he pushed his big red face into mine, and asked me what the hell I meant by interferin' with him.

'You tellin' me a white man can't whip a nigger if he feels like it? You sayin' there's some law against it?'

'Well,' I said. 'I don't know about that. I ain't saying there is, and I ain't saying there ain't. But there's a law against disturbin' the peace, and that's what you're doin'.'

'And what about him disturbin' my peace? How about that, huh? A god-danged stinkin' nigger almost knocking me off the sidewalk and making me spill my shotgun shells!'

'Well, now, there's some division of opinion about that,' I said. 'It looks like maybe you might have bumped into him instead of him bumpin' you.'

Tom yelled that what was the god-danged difference, any-ways? It was a nigger's place to look out for a white man and keep out of his way. 'Just ask anyone,' he said, looking around at the crowd. 'Ain't that right, fellas?'

Someone said, 'That's right, Tom,' and there was a little murmur of agreement. A kind of half-hearted murmur, because no one liked Tom very much even if they did have to side with him against a colored fella.

It looked to me like they'd really rather be on my side. All I had to do was change the issue a little, make it between me and him instead of between a white man and a black.

'Where did you get that board you been beating him with?' I said. 'It looks to me like it came out of the sidewalk.'

'So what if it did?' Tom said. 'You expect me to use my fists on a nigger?'

'Now, never you mind about that,' I said. 'The point is, you got no right to beat him with city property. Suppose you broke that board, then what? Why these good taxpayers here has got to pay for a new one. Suppose someone comes along and steps in that empty place in the sidewalk? These taxpayers has got to pay the damages.'

Tom scowled and cussed, and glared around at the crowd. There wasn't hardly a friendly face among 'em, so he cussed some more and said all right, then, to hell with the board. He'd just get the harness straps from his horse and beat Uncle John with them.

'Uh-huh,' I said. 'I don't reckon you will. Not right now, anyways.'

'Who's gonna stop me? What the hell you mean I won't do it right now?'

'I mean Uncle John ain't here right now,' I said. 'Kind of 'pears like he got tired of waitin' for you.'

Tom's mouth gaped open, and he looked around wildly. Everybody began to laugh, because naturally Uncle John had skipped out, and the expression on Tom's face was a sight to see.

He cussed me; he cussed the crowd. Then, he jumped on his mare and rode away, heeling her so hard in the flanks that she screamed with pain.

I stomped the sidewalk board back in place. Robert Lee Jefferson, the owner of the hardware store, caught my eye and motioned me to come inside. I went in, and followed him back to his little office.

Robert Lee Jefferson was the county attorney as well as the store owner, there not being enough work in the job to interfere with his business. I sat down, and he told me I'd handled the situation with Tom Hauck real well, and that Tom would surely have a lot of respect for law and order from now on.

'In fact, I imagine the whole town will, don't you, Nick? All those noble taxpayers who observed the manner in which you maintained the peace.'

'I guess you mean just the opposite of what you're sayin',' I said. 'Just what do you think I should have done, Robert Lee?'

'Why, you should have arrested Hauck, of course! Thrown him in jail! I'd have been delighted to prosecute him.'

'But what could I arrest him for? I sure couldn't do it for whippin' a colored fella.'

'Why not?'

'Aw, now,' I said. 'Aw, now, Robert Lee. You don't really mean that, do you?'

He looked down at his desk, hesitating a moment. 'Well, maybe not. But there are other charges you could have got him on. Being drunk in a public place, for example. Or hunting out of season. Or wifebeating. Or, uh—'

'But Robert Lee,' I said. 'Everyone does those things. A lot of people, anyways.'

'Do they? I haven't noticed any of them being brought into court for prosecution.'

'But I can't arrest everyone! Pretty near everyone.'

'We're talking specifically about one man. One mean, no-good, drunken, shiftless, lawbreaking wife-beater. Why didn't you make an example out of him for other men of his type?'

I said I just didn't rightly know, since he put it that way. I just didn't know; but I'd do some studyin' about it, and if I came up with an answer I'd tell him.

'I already know the answer,' he said curtly. 'Everyone with a lick of sense knows it. You're a coward.'

'Now, I don't know as I'd say that,' I said. 'I ain't sayin' that I ain't a coward, but—'

'If you're afraid to do your job by yourself, why don't you hire a deputy? The county provides funds for one.

'Why, I already got a deputy,' I said, 'my wife. I deputized Myra, so's she could do my office for me.'

Robert Lee Jefferson stared at me grimly.

'Nick,' he said, 'do you honestly think you can go on doing as you've been doing? Absolutely nothing, in other words. Do you really think you can go on taking graft and robbing the county, and doing nothing to earn your money?'

'Why, I don't see how I can do much else if I want to stay in office,' I said. 'I got all kinds of expenses that fellas like you and the county judge and so on ain't bothered with. Me, I'm out in the open all the time, brushin' up with hundreds of people whereas you folks only see one once in a while. Anyone that's put in trouble, why I'm the fella that puts 'em there; they don't see you until afterward. Anyone that needs to borry a dollar, they come to me. All the church ladies come to me for donations, and—'

'Nick . . .'

'I throw a big barbecue every night the last month before election. Come one, come all. I got to buy presents when folks has a new baby, and I got to—'

'Nick! Nick, listen to me!' Robert Lee held up his hand. 'You don't have to do all those things. People have no right to expect them of you.'

'Maybe they don't have a right,' I said. 'I'll go along with that. But what they got a right to expect, and what they do expect ain't exactly the same thing.'

'Just do your job, Nick. Do it well. Show people that you're honest and courageous and hard-working, and you won't have to do anything else.'

I shook my head, and said I couldn't. 'I just plain can't, Robert Lee, and that's a fact.'

'No?' He leaned back in his chair. 'And just why can't you, pray tell?'

'For a couple of reasons,' I said. 'For one thing, I *ain't* real brave and hard-workin' and honest. For another, the voters don't want me to be.'

'And just how do you figure that?'

'They elected me, didn't they? They keep electing me.'

'That's pretty specious thinking,' Robert Lee said. 'Perhaps they trusted and liked you. They've been giving you every chance to make good. And you'd better do it very quickly, Nick.' He leaned forward and tapped me on the knee. 'I'm telling you that as a friend. If you don't straighten up and do your job, you'll be out of it come fall.'

'You really think Sam Gaddis is that strong, Robert Lee?'

'He's that strong, Nick. Every bit that strong. Sam is just about everything you're not, if you'll excuse my saying so, and the voters like him. You'd better get busy or he'll beat the pants off of you.'

'Uh-*hah*!' I said. 'Umm-*humm*! Would you mind if I used your phone, Robert Lee?'

He said go ahead and I called Myra. I told her I was going out to Rose Hauck's place to help her do her chores, so that Tom wouldn't beat her up when he got home. Myra said that was just fine, her and Rose being such good friends – or so she thought – and she told me to stay as long as I liked.

I hung up the phone. Robert Lee Jefferson was staring at me like I was plumb out of my mind. 'Nick,' he said, waving his hands, 'haven't you heard a word I said? Is that your idea of doing your job – to go out and chore around the Hauck farm?'

'But Rose needs help,' I said. 'You surely ain't sayin' it's wrong to help her.'

'Of course, I'm not! It's nice of you to want to help her; that's one of your good qualities, the way you're always willing to help people. But – but—' He sighed and shook his head wearily. 'Aaah, Nick, don't you understand? It isn't your job doing things like that. It isn't what you're paid for. And you've got to start doing what you're paid for, or Sam Gaddis will beat you!'

'Beat me?' I said. 'Oh, you mean the election?'

'Of course I mean the election! What the hell else have we been talking about?'

'Well, I've been thinking about that,' I said. 'I've been doing a lot of thinking about it, Robert Lee, and I think I've thought of an angle that will beat ol' Sam.'

'An angle? You mean some kind of trick?'

'Well, you might call it that,' I said.

'B-But – but—' He looked like he was about to explode again. 'But why, Nick? Why not simply do your job?'

'Well, I thought a lot about that, too,' I said. 'Yes, sir, I really did a lot of thinking. Almost had myself convinced for a while that I actually should get out and start arrestin' people, and start actin' like a sheriff in general. But then I did some more thinkin', and I knew I hadn't ought to do nothing of the kind.'

'But, Nick—'

'Because people don't want me to do that,' I said. 'Maybe they think they do, but they don't. All they want is for me to give 'em some excuse to vote for me again.'

'You're wrong, Nick.' Robert Lee wagged his head. 'You're dead wrong. You've got away with tricks in the past, but they won't work this time. Not against a truly fine man like Sam Gaddis.'

I said, well, we'd just have to wait and see, and he gave me a sharp look.

'Have you got some idea that Sam Gaddis isn't a good man? Is that it, Nick? I can tell you right now that if you have some idea of digging up some dirt on him—'

'I got no such idea,' I said. 'I couldn't dig up no dirt on Sam if I wanted to, because there just ain't none to dig.'

'Good. I'm glad you realize that.'

'No, sir,' I said. 'I know Sam's as good a man as they come.

That's why I can't understand how all these stories about him got started.'

'Well, that's fine. I – *what*?' He stared at me startled. 'What stories?'

'You mean you ain't heard?' I said.

'Of course, I haven't! Now just what are these stories?'

I made as if I was about to tell him, and then I stopped and shook my head. 'I ain't gonna repeat 'em,' I said. 'If you ain't heard 'em, you sure ain't gonna hear 'em from me. No, siree!'

He took a quick look around and leaned forward, voice lowered. 'Tell me, Nick. I swear I won't repeat a word you say.'

'I can't. I just can't, Robert Lee. It wouldn't be fair, and there's just no reason to. What difference does it make if people are going around spreading a lot of dirty stories about Sam, as long as we know they're not true?'

'Now, Nick—'

'I tell you what I *am* gonna do,' I said. 'When Sam gets up to make his first campaign speech, come Sunday-week, I'm gonna be right up on the platform with him. He gets my moral support a thousand per cent, and I'm gonna say so. Because I know there ain't a word of truth in all them dirty, filthy stories that are going around about him!'

Robert Lee Jefferson followed me to the front door, trying to get me to say what the stories were. I kept refusing, naturally, the main reason being that I'd never heard no one say a bad word about Sam Gaddis in my life.

'No, sir,' I said, as I went out the door. 'I just ain't gonna repeat 'em. You want to hear any dirt about Sam you'll have to get it from someone else.'

'Who?' he said eagerly. 'Who should I ask, Nick?'

'Anyone. Just about anyone,' I said. 'There's always folks that are willin' to dirty a good man, even when they ain't got a thing to go on!'

got my horse and buggy out of the livery stable, and drove out of town. But I was quite a little while in getting out to see Rose Hauck. I had a little business with Tom to take care of first, business that was kind of a pleasure, if you know what I mean, and it was about an hour's drive to his favourite hunting place.

He was there, maybe a hundred feet back from the road, and he was doing his usual kind of hunting. Sitting with his back against one tree and his gun against another, and slugging down whiskey from a jug as fast as he could swallow.

He looked around as I came up on him, and asked me what the hell I was doing there. Then, his eyes widened and he tried to get to his feet, and he asked me what the hell I thought I was doing with his gun.

'First things first,' I said. 'One thing I'm doin' out this way is to pay a visit to your wife. I'm gonna be gettin' in bed with her pretty soon now, and she's gonna be givin' me what you were too god-danged low-down mean to ever get from her. Reason I know she's gonna give it to me is because she's been doin' it for a long time. Just about every time you were out here hog-drunk, too stupid to appreciate what a good thing you had.'

He was cussing before I had the last words out; pushing himself up against the tree-trunk, and at last wobbling to his feet. He took a staggering step toward me, and I brought the gun up against my shoulder.

'The second thing I'm gonna do,' I said, 'is somethin' I should have done long ago. I'm gonna give you both barrels of this shotgun right in your stupid, stinking guts.'

And I did it.

It didn't quite kill him, although he was dying fast. I wanted him to stay alive for a few seconds, so that he could appreciate the three or four good swift kicks I gave him. You might think it wasn't real nice to kick a dying man, and maybe it wasn't. But I'd been wanting to kick him for a long time, and it just never had seemed safe until now.

I left him after a while, getting weaker and weaker. Squirming around in a pool of his own blood and guts. And then ceasing to squirm.

Then, I drove on out to the Hauck farm.

The house was pretty much like most farm houses you see in this part of the country, except it was a little bigger. A pitched-roofed shack, with one long room across the front and a three-room lean-to on the back. It was made of pine, naturally, and it wasn't painted. Because with the hot sun and high humidity, you can't hardly keep paint on a house down here. At least, that's what folks say and even if it ain't so, it's a danged good excuse for being shiftless. The farm land, a whole quarter section of it, was as good as you'd find.

It was that rich, black silt you see in the river lowlands; so fine and sweet you could almost eat it, and so deep that you couldn't wear it out, like so much of the shallow soil in the south is worn out. You might say that land was a lot like Rose, naturally good, deep down good, but Tom had done his best to ruin it like he had her. He hadn't done it, because they'd had too much good stuff to begin with. But both the land and her were a long sight from being what they'd been before he got ahold of 'em.

She was hoeing sweet potatoes when I arrived, and she came

running up from the field, panting for breath and pushing the sweatsoaked hair from her eyes. One heck of a pretty woman, she was; Tom hadn't been able to change that. And she had one heck of a figure. Tom hadn't been able to ruin her body either, although he'd sure tried hard. What he had changed was the way she thought – mean and tough – and the way she talked. When she didn't have to be on guard, she talked practically as bad as he did.

'Goddam, honey,' she said, giving me a quick little hug and stepping back again. 'Dammit, sweetheart, I won't be able to stop today. That son-of-a-bitch of a Tom gave me too much work to do.'

I said, 'Aw, come on. You can spare a few minutes. I'll help you afterwards.'

She said, goddamn', it wouldn't do any good if she had six men to help her. She still couldn't get through. 'You know I want you, honey,' she said. 'I'm crazy about you, baby, and you know I am. If it wasn't for all this goddam work—'

'Well, I don't know,' I said, deciding to tease her along a while. 'I guess I ain't real sure that you do want me. Seems like as if you did, you could give me a minute or two.'

'But it wouldn't be a minute or two, darling! You know it wouldn't!'

'Why not?' I said. 'It don't take no longer than that to kiss you a little, and give you a few squeezes and pats, an'—'

'D-Don't!' She moaned shakily. 'Don't say those things! I—'

'Why, I'd probably even have time to hold you on my lap,' I said. 'With your dress sort of pulled up, so's I could feel how warm and soft you are where you sit down. And I could maybe sort of pull your dress down from the top, kind of slide it down from your shoulders, so that I could see those nice things underneath, and—'

'Stop it, Nick! I – you know how I get, a-and – I can't! *I just can't honey!*'

'Why, I wouldn't even expect you to take your dress all the

way off,' I said. 'I mean, it ain't really necessary, when you get right down to cases. With a tight-packed little gal like you, a fella don't have to do hardly nothing at all except—'

She cut me off, groaning like a spurred horse. She said, 'Goddam! I don't give a damn if the son-of-a-bitch beats my tail off!'

Then, she grabbed me by the hand and began to run, dragging me toward the house.

We got inside, and she slammed the door and locked it. She stood leaning into me for a moment, twisting and writhing against me. Then, she flung herself down on the bed, rolled over on her back and hitched her dress up.

'What the hell you waiting for, honey?' she said. 'Come on, darling, goddam it!'

'What you layin' down for?' I said. 'I thought I was just goin' to hold you on my lap.'

'P-Please, Nick!' She moaned again. 'We've g-got no time to waste, so – *please*, honey!'

'Well, all right,' I said. 'But I got some news for you. Sort of a little secret. I think maybe I ought to tell it to you before—'

'Crap on the secret.' She made a wild grab for me. 'I don't want any goddam secrets! What I want is—'

'But it's about poor old Tom. Somethin' done went and happened to him . . .'

'Who gives a damn? It's just too goddam bad that the son-of-a-bitch isn't dead! Now—'

I told her that that was the secret: Tom *was* dead. 'Looks like he got his guts blowed clear through his backbone,' I said. 'Looks like he stumbled over his gun when he was drunk, and blowed himself to glory.'

She looked at me, her eyes widening, mouth working as she tried to speak. Finally, the words came out in a shaky whisper:

'You're sure, Nick? You really killed him?'

'Let's just say he had himself an accident,' I said. 'Let's just say that fate dealt him a crool blow.'

'But he *is* dead? You're sure about that?'

I told her I was sure, all right. Plenty sure. 'If he ain't, he's the first live man I've ever seen who could hold still while he was getting kicked in the balls.'

Rose's eyes lit up like I'd given her a Christmas purty. Then she threw herself back on the pillows, rocking with laughter.

'Holy Jesus, so the stinking son-of-a-bitch is really dead! I'm through with the dirty bastard at last!'

'Well, sir, it sure looks that way,' I said.

'Goddam him! I just wish I'd have been there to kick him myself, the bastardly son-of-a-bitchin' whoremonger!' she said, adding on a few more choice names. 'You know what I'd have liked to do to that dirty bastard, Nick? I'd have liked to take me a red hot poker and jabbed it right up the filthy son-of-a-bitch's – uh, what's the matter, honey?'

'Nothin',' I said. 'I mean, maybe we ought to show a little more respect for ol' Tom, him bein' dead and all. It just don't seem quite fittin' to low-rate the dead with a lot of dirty names.'

'You mean I shouldn't call the son-of-a-bitch a son-of-a-bitch?'

'Well, now, it don't sound real good, does it?' I said. 'It don't sound nice a-tall.'

Rose said it sounded just fine to her, but if it bothered me she'd try to watch her tongue. 'That son-of-a-bitch caused enough trouble while he was alive without fouling us up afterward. Anyway, I'd do anything to please you, sweetheart. Anything you want, darling.'

'Then, why ain't you doin' it?' I said. 'How come you still got your dress on?'

'Goddam,' she said, looking down at herself. 'Rip the goddam thing off, will you, honey?'

I started ripping, and she started helping me with my clothes. And things were getting right to the most interesting point when the phone rang. Rose cussed and said to let the goddam thing go, but I said it might be Myra – which it was – so she stalked out in the kitchen and answered it.

She talked quite a while. Or, rather, she listened to Myra talking. About all Rose got to say was a lot of well-I-declare's and you-don't-say-so's and so on. Finally, she said, 'Why, of course I'll tell him, Myra, dear. Just as soon as he comes in from the field. And you and Lennie take care of your sweet selves until I see you again.'

Rose slammed up the phone, and came back to where I was. I asked her what Myra wanted, and she said it could wait, goddam it. There were more important things to do right now.

'Like what?' I said.

'Like this,' she said. '*This!*'

So we didn't do no talking for quite a while.

Not until afterwards, when we lay side by side, holding hands and breathing in long deep breaths. Then, finally, she turned around facing me, her head propped up on her elbow, and told me about Myra's call.

'Looks like a day for good news, honey. First, that son-of-a-bitch, Tom, gets killed, and now it looks like you're a cinch to get re-elected.'

'Yeah?' I said. 'How's that, baby?'

'Sam Gaddis. The whole town's talking about him. Why, do you know what he did, Nick?'

'I ain't got the slightest idea,' I said. 'I always thought Sam was a mighty good man.'

'He raped a little two-year-old nigger baby, that's what!'

'Mmmm? Male or female?' I said.

'Female, I guess. I – *ha, ha* – Nick, you awful thing, you.' She laughed and gave me a squeeze. 'But isn't it terrible, honey! To think of a grown man screwing a poor innocent little baby! And that's only one thing he did!'

'Do tell,' I said. 'Like which?'

Rose said that Sam had also cheated a poor widow woman

63

out of her life's savings, and then he'd beat his own father to death with a stick of cordwood to keep him from talking about it.

'And that's only the beginning. Nick. Everyone's saying that Sam broke into his grandma's grave, and stole the gold teeth out of her mouth. Did you ever hear of such a thing? And he killed his wife and fed her corpse to the hogs. And—'

'Now, wait a minute,' I said. 'Sam Gaddis has never been married.'

'You mean you just never saw his wife. He was married before he came here, and he fed her to the hogs before anyone could find out about her.'

'Aw, come on, now,' I said. 'Just when is Sam supposed to have done all these things?'

Rose hesitated and said, well, she didn't know when exactly. But, by God, she knew he'd done 'em.

'People wouldn't just make up stories like that. They couldn't!'

'Couldn't they?'

'Why, of course not, honey! Anyway, most of the stories came right from Mrs Robert Lee Jefferson, according to Myra. Her own husband told them to her, and you know Robert Lee Jefferson wouldn't lie.'

'Yeah,' I said. 'It don't seem like he would now, does it?'

And I had to bite my lip to keep from laughing. Or maybe doing the opposite. Because it was really pretty god-danged sad, now, wasn't it? It was a god-danged sorry state of affairs.

Of course, it was all to the good for me. I'd thrown the bait to Robert Lee Jefferson, and he'd bit on it. He'd done just what I expected him to do – gone around, asking people what the stories about Sam were. Which had started them to asking other people. And before long, there were plenty of answers; the kind of stinking dirty dirt that people can always create for themselves when there ain't none for real.

And it made me kind of sad, you know? Really downright

sad. I couldn't help wishing that Robert Lee hadn't taken the bait, and started asking questions. Which, in turn, had started piling up the dirt around a fine man like Sam Gaddis.

Yes, sir, I really sort of wished things hadn't worked out this way. Even if it did ruin Sam and get me re-elected, which it was just about certain to do.

Unless something went wrong . . .

11

I t rained during the night, and I slept pretty good like I almost always do when it rains. Along about ten the next morning, when I was having a little second breakfast because I hadn't eaten much the first time but a few eggs and some pancakes and sausage, Rose Hauck called.

She'd been trying to reach me for quite a while, but hadn't been able to because of Myra's gossiping about Sam Gaddis. Myra talked to her for a couple of minutes, and then passed the phone to me.

'I'm afraid something's happened to Tom, Nick,' Rose told me – just as if she didn't know what had happened to him. 'His horse came home without him this morning.'

'Is that a fact?' I said. 'You think maybe I should go out and start looking for him?'

'Well, I just don't know, Nick,' she hesitated. 'If Tom is all right, he might be pretty mad if I sent the sheriff after him.'

I said that was for sure, all right. Tom didn't like anyone butting in on his affairs. 'Maybe he holed up somewhere on account of the rain,' I said. 'Maybe he's waitin' for it to dry up a little before he starts home.'

'I'll bet that's it,' she said, making her voice relieved. 'He probably didn't have cover for the mare so he sent her home by herself.'

'That's probably the way it was, all right,' I said. 'After all, he didn't tell you he was coming home last night, did he?'

'No, no, he didn't. He never tells me how long he's going to be gone.'

'Well, don't worry none about it,' I said. 'Not yet, anyways. If Tom ain't home by tomorrow. why then I'll start lookin' for him.'

Myra was making wild faces and motions, as if to say, what is it all about? I passed her the phone and there was some more jibber-jabbering, and she wound up asking Rose to come have supper with us. 'Now, you just must come, dear, because I've got all kinds of news to tell you. You can get a ride in with the mailman about four, and I'll have Nick drive you home afterward.'

She hung up, shaking her head and murmuring, 'Poor Rose. That poor, dear, sweet woman.'

I said, 'Why, Rose ain't poor, honey. That's a right good farm her and Tom has.'

'Oh, shut up!' she said. 'If you'd have been half a man, you'd have done something about Tom Hauck long ago! Put him in jail where he belongs instead of leaving him free to beat up that poor little helpless wife of his!'

'Why, I couldn't do that,' I said. 'I couldn't interfere between a man and his wife.'

'No, you couldn't. You couldn't do anything! Because you're *not* half a man!'

'Well, now I don't know about that,' I said. 'I ain't saying you're wrong, but I sure ain't saying—'

'Oh, shut up!' she said again. 'Lennie's more of a man than you are. Aren't you, Lennie, darling?' – she smiled at him – 'you're Myra's brave strong man, aren't you? Not an old cowardly calf like Nick.'

Lennie slobbered out a laugh, pointing a finger at me. 'Cowardly calf, cowardly calf! Sheriff Nick's a cowardly calf!'

I looked at him, and he stopped laughing and pointing. He turned real quiet, and kind of pale.

I looked at Myra, and her smile stiffened and faded. And she was almost as pale and silent as Lennie.

'N-Nick—' She broke the long silence with a trembly laugh. 'W-What's the matter?'

'Matter?' I said.

'The way you're looking. Like you were about to kill Lennie and me both. I – I never saw you look that way before.'

I forced a laugh, making it sound easy and stupid. 'Me? Me kill someone? Aw, now!'

'But – but you—'

'I guess maybe I was thinking about the election. Thinking maybe it wasn't a very good idea to be pokin' fun at me with the election comin' up.'

She nodded her head quickly, and frowned at Lennie. 'Of course, we'd never carry on like that in public. But – but probably it isn't a good idea. Even if we were just joking.'

I thanked her for her understandin', and started for the door.

She followed me for a step, still kind of anxious; shook up from the scare I'd accidently given her.

'I don't think you have to worry about getting elected, dear. Not with all the talk that's going on about Sam Gaddis.'

'Well, I never believe in takin' chances,' I said. 'I always figure a fella ought to lean over backwards and put his shoulder to the wheel, and not count his chickens until they're hatched.'

'Mrs Robert Lee Jefferson said her husband said that you said you didn't believe the stories about Sam Gaddis.'

'I don't. I don't believe a god-danged word of 'em,' I said.

'But – she also said that he said that you said you were going to speak up for Mr Gaddis. She said that he said that you said you were going to be on the speakers' platform with him come Sunday-week.'

I told her she'd spoken the truth, and that was a fact. 'You talk to her again, you tell her that when she said that Robert Lee said that I said I was going to speak up for Sam Gaddis, she was a thousand per cent right.'

'You fool!—' She caught herself. 'But Gaddis is running against you, dear. Why should you do anything for him?'

'Now, that's quite a question, ain't it?' I said. 'Yes, sir, that is *quite* a question. Reckon I'd tell you the answer if I didn't figure you'd have so much fun cypherin' it out.'

'But—'

'Reckon I'd better be rushing back to my office,' I said. 'No tellin' what's been happening while I was away.'

I went on down the stairs, pretending like I didn't hear her when she called to me. I went in my office and sat down with my boots up on the desk. And I slanted my hat over my eyes, and kind of dozed for a little while.

It was awfully peaceful. The mud was keeping most folks indoors, and the painters were taking the day off because of the wet, so there wasn't a lot of slamming and banging and calling back and forth from them. A fella could really rest for a change, and catch up the sleep that he didn't get at night.

I rested and slept until noon, when I went upstairs for dinner.

Myra had got over her scare, and was about back to normal. She looked at me and said she could see I'd had a very busy morning, and she hoped I wasn't wearing myself out.

'Well, I'm trying not to,' I said. 'A fella like me, with the whole county depending on him for law and order, has got to watch out for his health. Which sort of reminds me. About me takin' Rose Hauck home tonight—'

'You're going to do it!' Myra snapped. 'You're going to, so just don't try to get out of it!'

'But suppose Tom's there? Suppose he's mad about me bringin' his wife home, an' – an'—'

I squirmed, letting my eyes fall, but I could still see Myra glaring at me. At last she spoke, her voice shaky with hate and disgust.

'You – you thing, you! You miserable excuse for a man! I'll tell you this, Nick Corey! If Tom *is* there and you let him hurt Rose, I'll make you the sorriest man in the county!'

'Now, my goodness,' I said. 'My goodness gracious! You don't need to talk that way. I wouldn't stand by an' watch Rose get hurt.'

'Well, you'd better not! That's all I've got to say! You'd just better not!'

I started eating, with Myra shooting me a suspicious look now and then. After a while, I looked up and said I'd just thought of something else about Rose. Suppose Tom came home, after I left and wouldn't be around to protect her.

'He's bound to be pretty bad off,' I said. 'Stayin' away so long, he'll probably be twice as drunk and mean as he usually is. Makes me plumb shiver to think what he might do to Rose.'

'Well . . .' Myra hesitated, studying over what I'd said and not finding anything to fault me for. 'Well, I don't suppose it would look right for you to stay all night at the house. But—'

'Naw, I couldn't do that! I sure couldn't do that,' I said. 'Anyways, we don't know for sure when Tom's comin' home. Might be gone, two, three days. All we know is he's gonna be plenty hard to get along with when he does get back.'

Myra fumed and frowned, and said I should have done something about Tom long ago, and Rose wouldn't be in this position now. I said she was probably right, and it was just too bad we couldn't think of some way to give Rose some protection.

'Let's see,' I said. 'I wonder maybe if we could get her a watchdog, or—'

'You fool! Tom would kill it in a minute! He's killed every dog they ever had!'

'Mmm-hmm,' I said. 'God-dang if I didn't forget about that. Well, let's see, now. I'd know of just the thing if Rose was a different kind of person. More nervy, you know, instead of so meek and mild. But that's the way she is, so it just wouldn't do no good.'

'What wouldn't do no good! What are you talking about now?'

'Why, a gun,' I said. 'You know, one of them things you shoot with. But it sure wouldn't do no good with Rose, her bein' scared of her own shadder, so—'

'That's it!' Myra cut in. 'We'll get her a gun! She ought to have one anyway, a woman alone as much as she is.'

'But what good will it do?' I said. 'Rose wouldn't shoot no one to save her life.'

'I'm not so sure about that – not if her life was at stake. At any rate, she could point it. Make that big brute of a husband keep away from her.'

'Well, now, I just don't know about that,' I said. 'If you ask me—'

'I'm not asking you! I'm taking Rose out to get a gun this very day, so just finish your dinner and shut up!'

I finished eating, and went back down to my office. I rested and dozed some more, but not as good as I had in the morning. I was kind of puzzled with myself, you know, wondering why I'd wanted Rose Hauck to have a gun. Because, of course, I did want her to have one.

I tried to tell myself that it was just for her own protection, just in case someone tried to bother her. But I knew that wasn't my real reason. My real reason, I guessed, was something I hadn't quite figured out yet. It was part of something else, some plan-wishes I had for Myra and Lennie – and I hadn't quite figured out what they were either.

Maybe it don't seem to make sense for a fella to be doing things for a reason that he don't know about. But I reckon I've been doing it most of my life. The reason I went to see Ken Lacey, for example, wasn't the one I let on that it was. I'd done it because I had a plan for him – and you've seen what that plan was. But I didn't know it at the time I'd called on him.

I'd had kind of a goal, and I'd figured that a fella like Ken could be a lot of help in bringing it about. But just how I was going to use him I wasn't even halfway sure.

And it was the same situation now, with Rose and the gun.

All I knew was that they probably fitted into a plan for Myra and Lennie. But I didn't have no real idea of what the plan was; I purely didn't.

Except that it was probably pretty unpleasant . . .

Rose got to the courthouse around four o'clock that afternoon. I was on the lookout for her, and I got her in the office for a minute before she could go on upstairs.

She was looking prettier than I'd ever seen her, which was really saying something. She said she'd slept like a goddam baby all night long, and she'd woke up laughing, thinking about that son-of-a-bitch of a Tom being dead out in the mud somewheres.

'Did I do all right when I called up this morning, honey?' she whispered. 'It sounded like I was really concerned about the dirty bastard?'

'You did just fine,' I said. 'And looky, baby . . .'

I told her about the gun, how it would look like she was worried about Tom beating her up when he came back – which, you see, would prove she didn't know he was dead. And she kind of hesitated for a second, giving me a quick frowny look, but she didn't argue about it.

'Whatever you say, Nick, honey. If you think it's a good idea.'

'Well, it was actually Myra's,' I said. 'I just about had to go along with it, or it would have looked like I knew Tom wasn't coming back.'

Rose nodded and said. 'What the hell?', dismissing the subject. 'Maybe I can take a shot at you some time, if you're not real nice to me.'

'That time ain't never gonna come,' I said. And I gave her a quick hug and a squeeze, and she went on up the stairs.

She and Myra went out a little later to get the gun, and stayed out until after five.

A few minutes before six, Myra called me, and I closed the office and went upstairs to supper.

Myra did most of the talking, like she always did; shutting

me up whenever I said anything. About all Rose did was agree with her, putting in a word now and then about how wonderful and smart Myra was. And that was the same as usual, too. We finished eating. Myra and Rose started clearing up the dishes. Lennie looked at me to see if I was watching him – which I was, only he didn't know it – and then he made a sneak toward the door.

I cleared my throat to get Myra's attention, and jerked my head at Lennie. 'How about that, honey?' I said. 'You know what we agreed on.'

'What?' she said. 'What are you talking about now, for pity's sake?'

'About him goin' out at night,' I said. 'You know what he'll do, an' it just ain't a good idea with the election coming up.'

Myra said, 'Oh, pshaw. The boy's got to get a little air some time, doesn't he? You can't begrudge him that!'

'But we agreed that—'

'I did not! You just got me so mixed up I wasn't thinking what I was saying! Anyway Sam Gaddis is bound to be beat and you know it!'

'Well, I just don't see no use in taking chances,' I said. 'I—'

'Oh, shut up! Did you ever see such a man in your life, Rose? Is it any wonder that I'm half out of my mind from living with him?' Myra scowled at me, then turned to give Lennie a smile. 'You go right ahead, honey. Have a good time, but don't stay out too late.'

He went out, after a blubbery spiteful grin at me. Myra said I'd better go to my bedroom and stay if I couldn't make sense, which she was sure I couldn't, so that's what I did.

I stretched out on the bed, with the spread turned back so that my boots wouldn't soil it. The window was open, and I could hear the crickets singing, like they always do after a rain. Now and then a bullfrog would sound off with a loud *kerrumph*, like a bass drummer keeping time. Way off across town, someone was pumping water, *p-plump, whish, p-plump, whish* and you could hear some mother calling her kid, '*Henry Clay, oooh, Hen-ry Clay Houston! You come home now!*' And the smell of fresh-washed soil was in the air, just about the nicest smell there is. And . . . and everything was fine.

It was so god-danged nice and peaceful that I dozed off again. Yes, sir, I went to sleep, even though I hadn't had a real hard work day and I'd managed to catch up on my rest a little.

I guess I must have been asleep about an hour when I waked up to the sound of Myra yelling and Lennie bawling, and someone talking to 'em – Amy Mason speaking her mind in a way that almost put your teeth on edge. Soft, but firm and cutting, like only Amy could speak when she had her dander up. You knew you'd better listen to what she was saying, when Amy spoke that way; you'd better listen and take it to heart or it would be too god-danged bad for you.

I knew it was having its effect on Myra, in spite of her yelling and trying to set defiant. She began to kind of whimper and whine, saying that Lennie didn't mean anything by peeking in Amy's window – he was just curious about people. Amy said she knew exactly what he meant, and he'd better not try any of his nasty tricks again if he knew what was good for him.

'I've already warned your husband,' she said, 'and now I'm warning you, Mrs Corey. If I catch your brother at my window again, I'll take a horsewhip to him!'

'Y-You wouldn't dare!' Myra whined. 'And you just stop hurting him! Let go of the poor boy's ear.'

'Gladly,' Amy said. 'It makes my flesh crawl to touch him.'

I cracked the door open an inch or so, and looked out.

Myra had her arm around Lennie, who looked red-faced and mad and scared as she patted him on the head. Rose was standing next to her, trying to appear concerned and protective. But I knew, knowing her so well, that she was laughing inside, tickled pink to see Myra catching it for a change. As for Amy . . .

I swallowed hard, looking at her, wondering what I'd ever seen in Rose after I'd had someone like Amy.

Not that she was any prettier than Rose, or built any better. You just couldn't fault Rose on prettiness or build no matter who you stood her up against. The difference, I guess, was something that came from the inside, something that kind of grabbed hold of you right around the heart, that left its mark on you like a brand, so that the feel of her and the memory of her was always with you no matter where you strayed.

I came bursting out of the bedroom and looked around, putting a real surprised look on my face. 'What's going on here, anyways?' I said, not givin' anyone a chance to answer. 'Why, good evening, Miss Mason. Is they some kind of trouble?'

Amy said no, they was not no kind of trouble; kind of mimicking me, you know. 'Not now there isn't, Sheriff. The trouble's all settled. Your wife will tell you how to avoid any in the future.'

'My wife?' I gave Myra and Lennie a studyin' look, and turned back to Amy. 'Did my wife's brother do somethin', Miss Mason? You just tell me about it.'

'Of course, Lennie didn't do anything!' Myra snapped. 'He was just—'

'Is your name Miss Mason?' I said. 'Is it?'

'W-What? What?'

'I asked Miss Mason a question,' I said. 'In case you ain't heard, Miss Mason is one of the most prominent and respected young women in Potts County, and when I ask her somethin' it's because I know she'll tell the truth. So maybe you'd better not go contradictin' what she says.'

Myra's mouth dropped open. She turned from red to white, and then back to red again. I knew she'd probably give me all-heck when she got me alone, but for the present she wasn't talkin' back. She knew she just hadn't better, what with an election coming up and Amy being so generally well-thought-of. She knew that someone like Amy could cause an awful lot of trouble, if they took a notion, and an election year was no time for trouble.

So Myra didn't give me any trouble, much as she felt like it, and Amy was kind of pleased by the way I'd acted, and said she was sorry if she'd said anything hurtful. 'I'm afraid I lost my temper for a moment,' she smiled, a little stiffly. 'If you'll excuse me, I'll run along home.'

'I'll walk you home myself,' I said. 'It's too late at night for a young lady to be out by herself.'

'Now, that's not at all necessary, Sheriff. I—'

I said it certainly was necessary; me and my wife, we wouldn't have it no other way. 'That's right, ain't it, Myra? You insist on me seein' Miss Mason home, don't you?'

Myra said yes, her teeth practically clenched together.

I nodded and winked to Rose and she winked back at me; and Amy and me left.

She lived right there in town, so I didn't get out the horse and buggy like I might have if her home had been a far piece off. Anyway, I wanted to talk to her and I didn't want her pulling away from me. And it's just about impossible for a woman to be standoffish when you're walking her home through the mud on a dark night.

She had to listen when I started telling her how Myra had hooked me. She said she just wasn't interested and it wasn't any of her business, and that sort of thing. But she listened anyway, because she couldn't get out of it. And after a couple of minutes she stopped interruptin' and began to cling closer to me, and I knew she believed what I was saying.

On the porch of the house, she flung her arms around me and I put mine around her, and we stood there in the darkness for a little while, just holding onto each other. Then, she sort of pushed me away, and I couldn't see her expression, but somehow I knew she was frowning.

'Nick,' she said. 'Nick, this is terrible!'

I said, 'Yeah, I guess I have kind of messed things up, all right. I guess I've been nine kinds of fool, lettin' Myra scare me into marryin' her and—'

'That's not what I'm talking about. That could be solved with money, and I have money. But – but—'

'Then, what's botherin' you?' I said. 'What's so terrible, honey?'

'I – I'm not sure.' She shook her head. 'I know *what*, but I don't know why. And I'm not positive it would make any difference if I did know. I – can't talk about it now! I don't even want to think about it! I – Oh, Nick! *Nick!*'

She buried her face against my chest. I held her tighter, stroking her head and whispering that everything was all right, that nothing could be so very terrible as long as we were together again.

'Now, it just couldn't, honey,' I said. 'You just tell me what it is, and I'll show you it don't really amount to nothin' at all.'

She clung to me a little tighter, still not saying anything. I said, well, to heck with it; maybe we could save it for another time, when I didn't have to be in kind of a rush like I was tonight.

'You remember how I used to go night-fishin'?' I said. 'Well, I was thinkin' maybe I might go tomorrow night, and it'd be kind of a natural mistake if I should wind up here instead of the river, because you ain't so awful far from it.'

Amy sniffled, then laughed.

'Oh, Nick! There's just no one like you!'

'Well, I should hope not,' I said. 'The world'd be in a heck of a mess if there was.'

I said I'd see her the next night, just as soon as it was good and dark. She shivered against me, and said that would be fine.

'But do you have to go now, darling?'

'Well, I guess I kind of should,' I said. 'Myra'll be wonderin' what happened, and I got to see Miz Hauck home yet tonight.'

Amy said, 'Oh, I see. I'd almost forgotten about Rose.'

'Yeah, I got to take her home,' I said, kind of grumbling about it. 'Myra has done promised her I would.'

'Poor Nick!' Amy patted my cheek. 'Everyone's always imposing on him.'

'Aw, I don't really mind,' I said. 'After all, someone's got to take care of poor Miz Hauck.'

'How true! And isn't it fortunate that she has someone so willing to take care of her! You know, Nick, poor ol' Mrs Hauck seems to be bearing up remarkably well under her troubles. She looked positively blooming, like a woman in love, one might say.'

'Is that a fact?' I said. 'I can't say that I rightly noticed.'

'Come in for a while, Nick. I want to talk to you.'

'I guess we better let it wait until tomorrow night,' I said. 'It's kind of late, an'—'

'Now! Tonight, Nick.'

'But Rose – I mean, Miz Hauck – will be waiting.

'Let her. I'm afraid it's not the only disappointment she's in for. Now, come in!'

She flung the door open and went in, and I went in after her. Her hand gripped mine in the darkness, and she led me back through the house to her bedroom. And it was a funny thing, her saying she wanted to talk to me, because she didn't do no talking at all.

Or hardly any.

Afterwards, she lay back and yawned and stretched; kind of fidgeting because I never could see good in the dark, and I was slow in getting my clothes on.

'Will you please hurry a little, darling? I feel all nice and relaxed and drowsy, and I want to get to bed.'

'Well, you sure ain't got far to get,' I said. 'What was it you was wantin' to talk to me about, anyways?'

'About your grammar, possibly. You're no ignoramus, Nick. Why do you talk like one?'

'Just habit, I guess. Kind of a rut I've got into. English and grammar, I reckon, they're like a lot of things. A fella don't use 'em – he don't see no real demand for 'em – and pretty soon he loses the knack. Wrong is right for him, an' vicey versa you might say.

Amy's head shifted on the pillows, her eyes wide in her white face as she studied me.

'I think I know what you mean, Nick,' she said. 'In a way, I'm a victim of the same process.'

'Yeah?' I said, pulling on my boots. 'How you mean, Amy?'

'Or I'm beginning to be a victim,' she said. 'And, you know, darling, I rather like it.'

I stood up, tucking in my shirttails. 'Just what was you wantin' to say to me, Amy?'

'Nothing that can't wait until tomorrow night. In fact, I no longer think I'll have anything to say then.'

'But you said—'

'And I said some other things, too, darling. Possibly you weren't listening. Now, you run along now, and I do hope pore ol' Miz Hauck ain't too disappointed.'

'Yeah,' I said. 'I sure hope she ain't either.'

But I had an idea she was going to be.

12

The way I'd met Myra was at the state fair a few years ago. I was all dressed up like I always am when I go someplace, and even a god-danged fool could see I was doing plenty all right. Anyway, I reckon Myra seen it. And she didn't look so bad herself then; she'd gone to some pains to pretty herself up. And I didn't fight too hard when she latched herself onto me.

It was at this place where you throw balls at a colored fella's head, and if you hit him you won a prize. I was just doin' it because the fella that ran the place kept asking me to. It had seemed unobliging not to, but I sure didn't want to hit this colored man and I didn't. But I heard someone clapping her hands, and here was Myra, carrying on like I was the world's greatest pitcher.

'Oooh, I just don't see how you do it!' she said, simpering up at me. 'Would you throw some balls for me, please, if I give you the money?'

'Well, I'd kind of rather not, ma'am,' I said. 'If you don't mind excusin' me, I was just quitting myself.'

'Oh,' she said, kind of letting her face sag, which didn't require much of an effort if you know what I mean. 'I understand. Your wife is with you.'

'Naw, that ain't it,' I said. 'I ain't married, ma'am; I just don't want to throw at that colored fella, because it don't seem right somehow. It ain't rightly decent, you might say.'

'You're just saying that,' she pouted and simpered. 'It's your way of rebuking me for being forward.'

I said, naw, that wasn't it at all; I really felt like I said I did. 'I guess it's his job to get throwed at, but it ain't mine to do the throwin',' I said. 'Anyways, a fella'd be better off without a job than one like this. If he's got to get hit to live, he ain't got nothing worth living for.'

Myra put on a solemn face, and said she could see I was a really deep thinker. I said, well, I didn't know about that, but I was sure a thirsty one.

'Maybe I could offer you a lemonade, ma'am, seein' as how I can't favor you by throwing balls.'

'Well . . .' She twisted and twitched and twittered. 'You won't think I'm terribly forward if I say yes?'

'Why, you just said it, ma'am,' I said, leading her toward the pink lemonade stand. 'You just said yes, and I don't think nothing like that at all.'

And sure enough I didn't.

What I was thinking was that she must have buggers in her bloomers or a chigger on her figger, or however you say it. It looked to me like something had better be done about it pretty quick, or her pants would start blazing and maybe they'd set the fairgrounds on fire and there'd be a panic with thousands of people getting stomped to death, not to mention the property damage. And I couldn't think of but one way to prevent it.

Well, though, I didn't want to rush into things. There just wasn't any need to rush, as far as I was concerned, because I was getting married to Amy the next week and she'd taken good care to provide for me until then. So I stalled around, trying to decide whether I really ought to do the only thing I could think of to do. You might say it really wasn't my problem if Myra did set the fairgrounds on fire, with thousands of innocent women and children getting killed. Because I was from out of town, and I'm a great believer in local rights – you know, like State rights

– and Myra lived here in the city. Could be I might get into all kinds of trouble by interfering in a local problem, even if it was something that even a god-danged fool would be familiar with, and the local folks weren't doing nothing about it.

I took Myra to a few side shows, standing close to her while I tried to make up my mind. I took her on the merry-go-round and some other rides, helping her on and off and looking at her when her dress slid up, and so on and so forth. And god-dang if it wasn't long before I came to my decision.

Myra looked shocked when I whispered to her, almost as shocked as if I'd bought her a sack of popcorn.

'Why – why, I just wouldn't think of it!' She twisted and twitched. 'The very idea, going to a hotel with a strange man!'

'But I ain't strange,' I said, giving her a pinch. 'I'm built just like the rest of 'em.'

'Oh, you awful thing, you!' she giggled. 'You're just terrible!'

'Why, I ain't neither terrible,' I said. 'Anyways, it ain't fair to say I am without more knowledge on the subject.'

She giggled and blushed, and said she just couldn't go to a hotel. 'I just couldn't! I really couldn't.'

'Well, if you can't you can't,' I said, getting a little tired of it all. 'Far be it from me to urge you.'

'But – but we could go to my rooming house. No one would think anything of it if you just came up to my room for a little visit.'

We took a streetcar over to the place where she lived, a big white house a few blocks from the river. It was a very respectable place, from all appearances, and the people were too. And no one lifted an eyebrow when Myra said we were just going upstairs to clean up before we went out for supper.

Well, sir, I hardly touched that woman. Or, anyway, if I did touch her, I didn't do much more than that. I was ready to and rarin' to, and, well, maybe I did do a *little* something. But with all them clothes she had on, it was god-danged little.

All of a sudden, though, she pushed me off to the floor,

starting to bawl and sob so loud you could hear her in the next block. I picked myself up and tried to shush her. I asked her what the heck was the matter, and I tried to pat her and calm her down. She shoved me away again, setting up an even bigger racket.

I didn't know what the heck to do. Anyways, I didn't have time to do anything before a bunch of the other roomers came busting in.

The women hovered around Myra, trying to soothe her and talk to her. Myra kept bawling and shaking her head, not answering when they asked her what the matter was. The men looked at me, and kept asking me what I'd done to Myra. And it was just one of those situations where the truth won't do and a lie's no help. Which fortunately there ain't many of in this vale of tears.

The men grabbed ahold of me and began to bat me around. One of the women said she was going to call the police, but the men said no, they'd take care of me themselves. They'd give me what I deserved, they said, and there were plenty of men in the neighborhood to help 'em.

Well, I couldn't really blame 'em for thinking what they did. I'd've probably thought the same thing in their place, what with Myra bawling and her clothes being messed up, and me not being in very good shape neither. They figured I'd raped her, and when a fella rapes a gal in this part of the country, he hardly ever gets to the jail. Or, if he does, he don't stay there very long.

I figure sometimes that maybe that's why we don't make as much progress as other parts of the nation. People lose so much time from their jobs in lynching other people, and they spend so much money on rope and kerosene and getting likkered-up in advance and other essentials, that there ain't an awful lot of money or man-hours left for practical purposes.

Howsoever, it sure looked like I was about to be the guest of honor at a necktie party, when Myra decided to speak up.

'I'm s-sure Mr Corey didn't mean to do wrong,' she said,

looking around teary-eyed. 'He's really a fine man, I'm sure, and he didn't mean to do wrong, did you, Mr Corey?'

'No, ma'am, I sure didn't,' I said, running my finger around my collar. 'I positively didn't mean nothing like that, and that's a fact.'

'Then why did you do it?' a man frowned at me. 'This is hardly something that a person does accidentally.'

'Well, I don't know about that,' I said. 'I wouldn't say you're wrong, but I ain't sure you're right either.'

He started to take a swing at me. I ducked but another fella caught me by the shoulder and flung me toward the door. I went down on my knees and someone kicked me, and some others jerked me to my feet again, not being very gentle about it, and then everyone was hustling me out of the room and trying to sock me at the same time.

Myra said, 'Wait! Please wait! It's all a mistake.'

They slowed down a little, and someone said, 'Now, don't upset yourself, Miss Myra. This skunk isn't worth it.'

'But he wants to marry me! We were going to get married tonight!'

Everyone was pretty surprised, including me, and they were puzzled too, which I wasn't. It looked like I'd sold my pottage for a mess of afterbirth, as the saying is. I'd been chasing females all my life, not paying no mind to the fact that whatever's got tail at one end has teeth at the other, and now I was getting chomped on.

'That right, Corey?' A fella nudged me. 'You and Miss Myra getting married?'

'Well,' I said. 'Well, it's like this, or at least that's the way I see it. I mean, uh—'

'Oh, he's so bashful!' Myra laughed. 'And he gets excited so easily! That's what happened when—' She looked down at herself, blushing and brushing at her mussed-up clothes. 'He got so excited when I said yes, I'd marry him, that – that—'

The women put their arms around her and kissed her.

The men slapped me on the back, and began shaking my hands. They said they were sorry they'd misunderstood the situation; and doggone it, couldn't a woman get a man in a heck of a lot of trouble without even halfway trying?

'Why, we might have had you strung up by the neck, Corey, if Miss Myra hadn't set things straight! Now, wouldn't that have been a fine state of affairs?'

'Yeah,' I said. 'That would have been a good joke on me. But looky, fellas. About this marriage business—'

'A wonderful institution, Corey. And you're getting a wonderful woman.'

'And I'm getting a wonderful man!' Myra jumped up and threw her arms around me. 'We're getting married right tonight, because Mr Corey just can't wait, and you're all invited to the wedding!'

It just happened that there was a preacher right up in the next block, so that's where we went – where everyone else went, I should say – and I got took. Myra dragged me along, with her arm hooked through mine; and those other folks brought up the rear, laughing and joking and slapping me on the back, and crowding on my heels so that I couldn't slow down.

I tried to sort of hang back, and they thought that was funny as all-heck. They thought the expression on my face was funny, and they practically went into hysterics when I said something like what was the god-danged hurry, and maybe we ought to think this over for a while.

It reminded me of one of those ceremonies you read about in ancient histories. You know. There's this big procession, with everyone laughing and carrying on and having themselves a heck of a time, and up at the head of it is this fella that's going to get sacrificed to the gods. He knows he'll get his ass carved up with a meat axe as soon as they stop throwing roses at him, so he sure ain't in no hurry to get to the altar. He can't get out of the deal, but neither can he put his heart into it. And the more he protests, the more people laugh at him.

So . . .

So that's what it reminded me of. A fella getting sacrificed for something that just ain't worth it.

But I guess a lot of marriages strike me the same way. Everything for show and nothing for real. Everything for public and nothing for private.

And that night, after me and Myra were in bed – I guess a lot of marriages turn out like that, too. Bawling and accusations and mean talk: the woman taking it out on the man because he was too stupid to get away from her.

Or maybe I'm just kind of sour . . .

13

I got my horse and buggy out of the livery stable, and drove back to the courthouse. Myra was jumping on me, wanting to know what had took me so long, almost as soon as I was inside the door. And I said I'd had quite a time getting things straightened out with Amy.

'I don't see why,' Myra said. 'She seemed calm enough when she left here.'

'Well, there's quite a few things you don't see,' I said. 'Like why you should keep Lennie in at night so we wouldn't have messes like this.'

'Now, don't you start in on Lennie!'

'I tell you what I'd like to start,' I said. 'I'd like to start home with Rose, so maybe we could all get to bed sometime tonight.'

Rose said yes, she really should be going, and she thanked Myra for the dinner and hugged her and kissed her good night. I went on downstairs ahead of her, before I got into another argument, and she came running down after a minute of two and got into the buggy.

'Ugh!' she said, scrubbing at her mouth. 'Every time I kiss that old bitch I want to wash out my mouth.'

'You ought to watch that cussing, Rose,' I said. 'It's liable to slip out sometime when you don't mean it to.'

'Yeah, I guess I should, goddam it,' she said. 'It's Tom's fault, the dirty son-of-a-bitch, but I'm sure as hell going to do my best to stop it.'

'That's my girl,' I said. 'I can see you ain't going to have no trouble.'

We were outside of town by now, and Rose moved over in the seat to snuggle up against me. She kissed me on the back of my neck and she put a hand inside my pocket and sort of wiggled it around; and then she kind of moved away a little, and gave me a funny look.

'What's the matter, Nick?'

'What?' I said. 'How's that, Rose?'

'I said, what's wrong with you?'

'Why, nothing,' I said. 'Course I'm kind of tired and wore out from all the excitement tonight, but there ain't nothing really wrong.'

She stared at me, not saying anything. She turned around in the seat, facing straight ahead, and we rode in silence for a while. At last she spoke, in a voice so low I could hardly hear it, asking me a question. I went cold all over, and then I said, 'For gosh's sake! What a thing to say! You know Amy Mason ain't that kind of woman, Rose! Everyone knows she ain't.'

'What the hell you mean she's not that kind?' Rose snapped. 'You mean she's too goddam good to go to bed with you, but I'm not?'

'I mean, I just ain't hardly acquainted with the woman!' I said. 'I barely know her to tip my hat to.'

'You were gone long enough tonight to get acquainted!'

'Aw, naw, I wasn't, honey,' I said. 'It just seemed like a long time to you, like it did to me. You know. Because we were just waitin' to get together tonight, and it seemed like a heck of a long wait. Why, honey, I was just itchin' and achin' for you from the minute you showed up today.'

'Well . . .' She moved over a little in the seat.

'Why, for gosh's sake,' I said. 'What for would I want with Amy Mason when I got you? Why, it just don't make sense, now does it? There just ain't no comparison between the two of you!'

Rose came all the way over in the seat. She leaned her head against my shoulder, and said she was sorry, but I had acted kind of strange, and it did make her so goddam mad the way some men were.

'That goddam Tom, for example! The son-of-a bitch just wouldn't leave me alone until I gave in to him, and then he goes out and screws everything that can't outrun him!'

'Tsk, tsk,' I said. 'I just can't understand fellas like that.'

Rose squeezed me and kissed me on the ear. She gave me a little nibble on the ear, and whispered to me. Talking about what-all she was going to do to me when we got to her house.

'Myra wants you to stay a while, and make sure I'm all right. Isn't that nice, mm? We can take our time, just you and me together for hours and hours. And, honey, we won't waste a minute of it!'

'Oh, boy,' I said.

'It'll be like it never was before, darling!' She shivered against me. 'Oh, honey, I'm going to be something special for you tonight!'

'Goll-ee,' I said. 'Goody, gosh-dang.'

She went on whispering and shivering against me, saying that this was one night I'd never forget. I said I bet I wouldn't neither, and I meant every word of it. Because the way I was feeling, as hollow as a tree-bark whistle and like my back was broken in six places, there wasn't going to be no party when we got to Rose's house. Which meant that she'd know she'd been right about Amy. Which also meant that she'd probably take that gun she'd got today and shoot me right through the offendin' part. And with a memento like that, I sure wouldn't forget the night.

I tried to think of some way of stalling her. I looked up at the sky, which was clouding over again for a rain, and I saw a streak or two of lightning, and I thought, well, maybe a bolt would strike me, cold-cocking me for the night, so that Rose would excuse me. Then I thought, well, maybe the horse would run away and throw me into a bob-wire fence, and Rose would have to let me off then, too. Or maybe a water moccasin would climb up in the buggy and fang me. Or—

But nothing like that happened. A fella never gets lucky that way when he really needs to.

We reached the farm. I drove on into the barn, wondering how much it would handicap a fella having a hole where I was going to have one. It seemed to me it would mess him up pretty bad in the things he needed to do most, and I climbed down from the buggy, feeling mighty glum.

I helped Rose down, giving her a smack on the bottom by way of habit. Then, I bent down behind the splashboard to unhitch the singletree, and the horse was fidgeting and switching his tail and I was saying, 'Sooo, boy, soo, now.' And then I thought of an idea.

I gave the horse a goose and made him jump. I drove my shoulder against the splashboard, making a heck of a racket like the horse had kicked it. Then I jumped out in the clear again, groaning and clutching myself.

Rose came running up, clinging to me by one arm as I staggered around doubled over. 'Oh, honey! Darling! Did that goddam nag kick you?'

'Right in the you-know-what,' I groaned. 'I never had nothin' hurt so bad in my life.'

'Goddam him to hell, anyway! I'll get a pitchfork and gut the brindle bastard!'

'Naw, don't do nothin' like that,' I said. 'The horse didn't go to do it. Just help me get him hitched up again, so's I can get home.'

'Home? You're not going anywhere in your condition,' she said. 'I'm taking you in the house, and don't you argue about it.'

I said, but, looky, now, it wasn't necessary to go to all that trouble. 'I'll just go home and lay down with some cold towels on it, and—'

'You'll lie down here, and we'll see about the towels after I see what the damage is. It might be you need something else.'

'But, looky, looky here, now, honey,' I said. 'It's kind of private, a thing like that. It ain't hardly something a woman should deal with.'

'Since when?' Rose said. 'Now, come on and stop arguing with me. Just lean on me and we'll go real slow.'

I did what she said. There just wasn't anything else I could do.

We got to the house. She helped me back into the bedroom, made me lay down on the bed and started taking off my clothes. I told her she didn't need to take them all off, because the pain was just in the part that my pants covered. She said it wasn't any trouble at all, and I could relax better if I was all undressed instead of partways, and to stop butting into her business.

I said that it was my business that got hurt, and she said, well, my business was her business, and right now she was running the store.

She leaned down over the place where I was hurt, or supposed to be hurt, turning the lamp this way and that so that she could make a proper inspection.

'Hmmm,' she said. 'I don't see any bruises, honey. No breaks in the skin.'

I said, well, it sure hurt, that's all I knew. 'Of course a fella don't have to get hit very hard in that area to make him hurt to beat heck.'

She said, 'Let's see, now, you tell me here it hurts. Does it hurt *there*, or *here*, or *here*—'

She was awful gentle, so gentle that it wouldn't have hurt me in any of the places even if I *had* been hurt. I told her that maybe she'd better be a little more firm about it so I could make sure of where the pain was. So she pushed and pressed a little harder, asking if it hurt *there* or *here* and so on. And I let out an

'Ooh' or an 'Aah' now and then. But what I was feeling wasn't pain.

It didn't matter any more about Amy; me being with her that night, I mean. I was as ready and rarin' as I'd ever been, and, of course, Rose wasn't long in noticing the fact.

'Hey, now!' she said. 'Just what's going on here, mister?'

'What does it look like?' I said.

'It looks to me like a big business recovery.'

'Well, god-dang, gee-whillikins!' I said. 'And right after a severe blow to the economy! You reckon we ought to celebrate the occasion?'

'What the hell you think?' she said. 'Just let me get these goddam clothes off!'

I snoozed a little while afterwards. No more than fifteen minutes, probably, because I'd rested quite a bit that day and wasn't really tired.

I came awake with Rose's hand biting into my arm, her voice a scary whisper. '*Nick!* Nick, wake up! Someone's outside!'

'What?' I mumbled, starting to roll over on my side again. 'Well, leave 'em out there. Sure don't want 'em in here.'

'Nick! They're on the porch, Nick! What – who do you suppose it—'

'I don't hear nothin',' I said. 'Maybe it's just the wind.'

'No, it – *listen!* There it is again!'

I heard it then; faint, careful footsteps, like someone moving on tiptoe. And along with them, a dull craggy sound, as if something heavy was being dragged up on the stoop.

'N-Nick. What do you think we'd better do, Nick?'

I swung my legs off the bed, and said I'd get my gun and have a look. She started to nod, and then she put out her hand and stopped me.

'No, honey, it won't look right your being here this time of night. Not with the lights all off and your horse put away.'

'But I'll just take a little peek out,' I said. 'I won't show myself to no one.'

'You might have to. You just stay here and keep quiet, and I'll go.'

She slid quietly out of bed, and trotted into the other room, making no more noise than a shadow. I was pretty nervy, naturally, wondering who or what was up on the porch and what it might have to do with me and Rose. But the way she was taking things, sort of keeping out in front and leaving me in the background, was a big comfort. I thought about Myra's idea of Rose as someone meek and mild and ready to jump at her own shadow, and I almost laughed out loud. Rose could whip her weight in bobcats if she took a notion. She'd maybe let Tom get the best of her, but that just wasn't no way a fair match.

I heard the click of the key in the outside door.

I sat up, kind of poised on the edge of the bed, ready to move if she called to me.

I waited, holding my breath for quiet. There was another click, as Rose unlatched the screen, and then a rusty squeak as she pushed it open. Then . . .

It was a small house, like I've said. But from where I was to where she was was still quite a piece – maybe thirty feet or more. Yet that far away, I heard it. The gasp; the scared-crazy sound of her breath sucking in.

And then she screamed. Screamed and cussed in a way I don't ever want to hear again.

'N-Nick! Nick! The son-of-a-bitch is back! That goddam Tom's back!'

14

grabbed for my pants, but the legs were twisted and the way Rose was carrying on, I didn't have no time to fool with 'em. Pants weren't what I needed anyway, with that god-danged Tom back. So I snatched up my gun, which I sure as heck did need, and ran for the door.

I tripped over a chair in the kitchen, almost taking a header against the wall. I righted myself, and dashed out to the porch. Then, I saw how things were – and they sure weren't good, all right, but they were a lot better than I'd expected 'em to be.

It was Tom's body that was there, not Tom. It had been left on the porch, face up, with the shotgun placed at the side. The beard had grown out some, because hair does go on growing for a while on dead people. He was all covered over with mud, and the middle of his body was just a big gutsy hole. His eyes were wide open and staring. The meanness was gone from them, but the fear that had taken its place was worse. Whatever death looked like, it sure didn't look good to him.

All in all, you might say he wasn't a very pretty sight. Nothing that would take first prize in a best-lookin'-fella contest. Old man Death had painted Tom Hauck in his true colors, and it wasn't an even halfway flattering portrait.

I couldn't really blame Rose for carrying on like she was. Almost any woman would have done the same, if her husband had come home in the middle of the night looking like Tom did. Rose had a right to raise a ruckus, but it wasn't helping things, particularly helping me to think. Which I was obviously in need of doing and fast. So I got an arm around her and tried to calm her down.

'Easy, now, honey, easy. This don't look so good, but—'

'Goddam you, why didn't you kill him?' She tore away from me. 'You told me you killed the son-of-a-bitch!'

'I did, baby. He sure don't look like no live man, now does he? He couldn't be no more dead if—'

'Then who brought him back here? What goddam dirty bastard did it? If I get my hands on the son-of-a-bitch—'

She broke off and whirled around wild-eyed seeming to listen for something. I started to say I wanted to get my hands on the fella, too, because just why the heck had he done this anyway? Rose told me to shut my goddam mouth.

'Now, honey,' I said. 'That ain't no way to talk. We got to be calm and—'

'There!' she yelled, pointing. 'There he is! That's the son-of-a-bitch that did it!'

She leaped off the porch and started running. Racing up the lane that led from the house to the road. Her naked white body faded into the darkness. I hesitated, wondering if I shouldn't at least put my pants on, and then I thought what the heck, and I ran after her.

I couldn't see whatever Rose had seen. I couldn't hardly see nothing, it being so dark. But I did hear something – the squeak of wagon wheels and the soft plod-plod of horses' hooves on the muddy lane.

I kept running. Finally, the squeaking and the plodding stopped and I saw the white of Rose's body. Then, she was cussing and screaming again, ordering whoever it was to climb down off the wagon.

'Get down, you black bastard! Get down, goddam you! What the hell's the idea of bringing back that son-of-a-bitch of a husband of mine?'

'Miz Rose. Please, ma'am, Miz Rose. I—' It was the soft, frightened voice of a man.

'I'll show you, you son-of-a-bitch! I'll teach you! I'll peel your black ass right down to the bones!'

She was trying to tear loose a piece of harness strap when I ran up. I jerked her around, and she faced me wild-eyed, pointing shakily to the fella who stood at the side of the wagon.

It was Uncle John, the colored fella I mentioned earlier. He was standing with his hands half-raised, and in the darkness his frightened eyes seemed all whites. He kept them turned away, naturally, because a colored fella could get himself killed for looking at a naked white woman.

'H-He – he did it!' Rose began to bawl. 'He brought the son-of-a-bitch back, Nick!'

'Well, now, I'm sure he didn't mean no harm by it,' I said. 'Howdy do, Uncle John. Nice evenin'.'

'Thank you, Mistah Nick. I's feelin' tol'able thank you.' His voice shook with fear. 'Yes, suh, sho' is a fine evenin'.'

'You son-of-a-bitch!' Rose yelled. 'What'd you bring him back for? Why do you think we got rid of the dirty bastard, anyway?'

'Rose!' I said, '*Rose!*', and Uncle John's eyes rolled in his head and he said, 'Please, ma'am, Miz Rose.' and it sounded like a prayer.

He'd already seen a lot, a heck of a lot more than it was healthy to see. He sure didn't want to hear anything to go with it. Rose slipped away from me again, opening her mouth for another yell, and Uncle John tried to stopper his ears with his fingers. But he knew it was no good. He heard, and he knew that I knew it.

'It's not fair, Nick, goddam it! You go to all the trouble of killing the son-of-a-bitch, and this bastard brings him back!'

I slapped her across the mouth. She whirled and came at me, hands clawed. I grabbed her by the hair, lifted her off the ground, and gave her a criss-cross slap, backwards and forwards.

'You get the idea?' I said, letting her back down on her feet. 'Now, you shut up and get back to the house or I'll give you the worst beating you ever had in your life.'

Her hand went slowly to her face. She looked down at herself, seeming to realize for the first time that she was naked. Shivering, she tried to cover up with her hands, shooting a scared look at Uncle John.

'N-Nick. What – what'll we—'

'Go on, do what I told you to.' I gave her a push toward the house. 'Me an' Uncle John will handle this.'

'B-But – but why did he do it?'

'I got an idea about that, too,' I said. 'You run along, now, and everything will be fine.'

She hesitated, then scampered back up the lane. I waited until I was sure she was really gone, and then I turned around to Uncle John.

I smiled at him, and he tried to smile back. But his teeth were chattering so bad that he couldn't.

'Now, don't be scared, Uncle John,' I told him. 'You got nothin' to fear from me. Ain't I always treated you right, now, ain't I? Ain't I always done the very best I could by you?'

'Yes, yes, suh Mistah Nick,' he said eagerly, 'an' I done right by you, suh, ain't I, Mistah Nick? Now, ain't that the truth, suh? Ain't I been a plumb good nigger for you?'

'Well, sir,' I said, 'I reckon I could call you that, all right.'

'Yes, suh, Mistah Nick. Any of them bad niggers startin' trouble, I always comes an' tells you, suh. Any of 'em steal a chicken or shoot crap or get drunk or all 'em other things bad niggers do, I always comes right an' reports it to you, now don't I, suh?'

'Well, sir,' I said. 'I reckon you're right about that, too, and I ain't forgettin' it, Uncle John. But just what are you getting at anyways?'

He gulped and choked, swallowing a sob. 'Mistah Nick, I won't say nothin' about – 'bout what happen tonight. Hones',

Mistah Nick, I won't say nothin' to no one. You just let me go an'—an'—'

'Why, sure I will,' I said. 'Ain't keeping you from leaving now, am I?'

'Y-You really means it, Mistah Nick? You really ain't mad at me none? I c'n go home right now, an' just keep my big ol' mouth shut forevah an' evah?'

I told him that of course he could leave. But I'd feel a lot better if he first told me how he happened to be here with Tom Hauck's body.

'You don't do that, I might be kind of suspicious of you. I might figure you'd done something bad and was trying to hide it.'

'No, suh, Mistah Nick! Doin' something bad was jus' what I didn't! I try to do good, an' then I get all mixed up, ol' foolish me an' – an' – oh, Mistah Nick!' He covered his face with his hands. 'D-Don't be mad at me, suh. Uncle John, he don't know nothin' at all. He don't h-hear nothin' an' he don't see nothin', an' – an' – please don't kill me, Mistah Nick! Please don't kill ol' John.'

I patted him on the back, letting him cry for a minute. Then I said I knew he hadn't done nothing wrong, so why would I want to do anything bad to him. But I'd sure be obliged if he told me just what *had* happened.

'Y-You—' He uncovered his face to look at me. 'You really ain't gonna kill me, Mistah Nick? Honest?'

'God-dang it, you callin' me a liar?' I said. 'Now, you just start talkin', and don't you tell me nothing but the truth.'

He told me what had happened, why he had brought Tom Hauck's body back to his farm house.

It stacked up just about the way I thought it would.

He had come across the body early that evening while he was out hunting 'possum, and he'd started to come into town to tell me about it. Then, with so many varmints around, he figured it might be best to bring the body in with him. So he'd loaded it on his old spring wagon, along with the shotgun, and headed for town again.

He was about halfway there when it struck him that it might be a pretty bad idea to show up in town with the remains; in fact, it was a god-danged bad idea to be caught even in the same neighborhood with them. Because a lot of people might figure he had a first-class motive for killing Tom. After all, Tom had given him a hard beating and intended to beat him again if he got within grabbing range. He just couldn't lead a very happy life as long as Tom was around, so it wouldn't be any surprise at all if he killed him. Anyways, Uncle John being a colored fella, he wouldn't get the benefit of any doubts.

Tom Hauck was completely no good, and the community was well shet of him. But they'd still lynch Uncle John. It would sort of be their civic duty, the way they'd see it; part of the process of keeping the colored folks in hand.

Well, so poor old Uncle John had got himself in a pickle. He couldn't take Tom's body into town, or even be seen with it. And Tom being a white man, he couldn't bring himself to just dump the body off in a ditch somewhere. There was only one thing he could do, as he saw it; only one thing that would be acceptable to Tom's white ghost and the All-Knowing God that he had been taught to believe in. He'd just take the dead man back to his own home and leave him there.

'Now, don't that seem fittin', Mistah Nick? You see how I figgered, suh? I reckon now, it sho' wasn't the right thing to do, seein' as how Miz Rose carry on so bad, an'—'

'Well, now, don't you worry none about that at all,' I said. 'Miss Rose was just upset seeing her husband dead, and pretty ugly-dead, at that. It's probably goin' to take her quite a while to get over it, so maybe we'd better move the body somewheres else until then.'

'But – b-but you say I could leave, Mistah Nick. You say I jus' tell you the truth, an'—'

'Yes, sir, that's what we'd better do,' I said. 'So just you hurry up, and turn your wagon back around.'

He stood there, head bowed; his mouth working like he was trying to say something. There was a long roll of thunder, and then a jagged flash of lightning, lighting his face for a moment. And somehow I had to look the other way.

'You hear me, Uncle John?' I said. 'You hear what I tell you to do?'

He hesitated, then sighed and climbed up on the wagon. 'Yes, suh, I hear you, Mistah Nick.'

We drove back to the house. It began to rain while we were loading Tom's body, and I told Uncle John to stand on the porch until I was dressed so that he wouldn't get no wetter than he had to.

'You're probably kind of hungry,' I said. 'You want I should bring you a cup of hot chicory? Maybe a little pone or somethin'?'

'I reckon not, thank you, suh.' He shook his head. 'Miz Rose probably got no fire this time o' night.'

'Well, we'll just build one up,' I said. 'No trouble at all.'

'Thank you, suh, I guess not, Mistah Nick. I – I ain't real hongry.'

I went on in the house and dried off with a towel Rose gave me, and it sure felt good getting back into my clothes. She was pestering me with questions while I dressed: what were we going to do and what was I going to do, and so on. I asked her what she thought; did she reckon she'd ever feel safe with someone knowing what Uncle John knew.

'Well—' She wet her lips, her eyes turned away from mine. 'We can give him some money, can't we? Both of us will. That should, uh, well, he wouldn't want to say anything then, would he?'

'He takes a drink now and then,' I said. 'No tellin' what a fella will do when he gets enough booze in him.'

'But he—'

'And he's a very religious fella. Wouldn't be at all surprised if he figured he ought to pray for us.'

'You can send him away somewhere,' Rose said. 'Put him on a train and send him up north.'

'He can't talk up there? He wouldn't feel more free to do it away from us than he would here?'

I laughed and chucked her under the chin, asking her what she was so squeamish about. 'Here I thought you was a real tough woman. It didn't bother you at all about what happened to Tom.'

'Because I hated the son-of-a-bitch! It's not the same with Uncle John, a poor nigger man who was just trying to do the best he could!'

'Maybe Tom was doing the best he could, too. I wonder if we did any better.'

'But – but, Nick! You, why you know what the bastard was like.'

I said, yeah, I knew, but I'd never heard of anyone killing Tom's wife, and Tom sleeping before and after with the party that did it. Then, I laughed, cutting her off before she could butt in. 'But this is different all right, honey,' I said. 'This you know about before it happens. It ain't something you learn about afterwards, so you can say, well, what can I do about it, and it ain't really my doin'.'

'Nick—' She touched my arm, sort of frightened. 'I'm sorry I lost my head tonight, honey. I guess I can't blame you for trying to hurt me.'

'It ain't really that,' I said. 'I reckon I'm just kind of tired of doing things that everybody knows I'm doing, things they really want and expect me to do, and having to take all the blame for it.'

She understood; she said she did, anyway. She put her arms around me and held me for a little while, and we talked a couple of minutes about what would have to be done. Then I left because I had a pretty full night's work ahead of me.

I had Uncle John drive up in the back country, about three miles behind the farm. We unloaded Tom's body there, in the edge of some trees, and Uncle John and I took such shelter as we could a few feet away.

He sat down at the base of a tree, his legs being too wobbly to hold him up any longer. I hunkered down a few feet away from him, and broke open the barrel of the shotgun. It looked fairly clean, clean enough to be safe, anyways. I blew through it a couple of times to make sure, and then I loaded it with the shells I'd taken from Tom's pockets.

Uncle John watched me, all the begging and praying in the world in his eyes. I relatched the barrel, and sighted along it, and he began to cry again. I frowned at him, feeling pretty fretted.

'Now, what you want to carry on like that for?' I said. 'You knew what I was goin' to have to do right along.'

'No, s-suh, I believe you, Mistah Nick. You different f'm other white folks. I believe every word you say.'

'Well, now, I think you're lyin', Uncle John,' I said, 'an' I'm sorry to hear you. Because it's right in the Bible that lyin's a sin.'

'It's a sin to kill folks, too, Mistah Nick. Worse sin than lyin'. Y-You – you—'

'I'll tell you somethin' Uncle John,' I said. 'I'll tell you something, and I hope it'll be a comfort to you. Each man kills the thing he loves.'

'Y-You don't love me, Mistah Nick . . .'

I told him he was god-danged right about that, a thousand per cent right. What I loved was myself, and I was willing to do anything I god-dang had to to go on lying and cheating and drinking whiskey and screwing women and going to church on Sunday with all the other respectable people.

'I'll tell you something else,' I said, 'and it makes a shit-pot-ful more sense than most of the goddam scripture I've read. Better the blind man, Uncle John; better the blind man who pisses through a window than the prankster who leads him thereto. You know who the prankster is, Uncle John? Why, it's goddam near everybody, every son-of-a-bitch who turns his head when the crap flies, every bastard who sits on his dong with one thumb in his ass and the other in his mouth and hopes that nothing will happen to him, every whoremonger who thinks that piss will turn into lemonade, every mother-lover supposedly made in God's image, which makes me think I'd hate like hell to meet him on a dark night. Even you, particularly you, Uncle John; people who go around sniffing crap with their mouth open, and acting surprised as hell when someone kicks a turd in it. Yeah, you can't help bein' what you are, jus'a pore ol' black man. That's what you say, Uncle John, and do you know what I say? I say screw you. I say you can't help being what you are, and I can't help being what I am, and you goddam well know what I am and have to be. You goddam well know you've got no friends among the whites. You goddam well ought to know that you're not going to have any because you stink, Uncle John, and you go around begging to get screwed and how the hell can anyone have a friend like that?'

I gave him both barrels of the shotgun.

It danged near cut him in two.

15

What I wanted things to look like was that Uncle John had shot Tom with his own gun and then Tom had got the gun away from him and shot Uncle John. Or vice versa. Anyways, when I got to thinking about it afterward, it seemed to me that people weren't going to see it that way at all. Which meant that they were apt to start looking for the real killer. And for a spell there, I was pretty worried. But I didn't need to be. As plumb crazy as it was, with Uncle John getting killed almost two days after Tom and with both of 'em obviously dying almost the instant they was shot, it turned out no one thought anything of it. They didn't wonder at all about how one dead man could've killed another.

Of course, both bodies were wet and muddied up, so you couldn't say offhand just when they'd died; and we just ain't equipped to do a lot of scientific examination and investigation here in Potts County. If things look a certain way, folks usually figure that's the way they are. And if they'd had a mind to kick up a fuss about anyone, it wouldn't be Tom Hauck or Uncle John.

The plain fact was that no one much gave a good god-dang about either one of 'em. It was a plain case of good riddance to bad rubbish as far as Tom was concerned; and who cared about one colored fella more or less, unless it was some other colored folks, and who cared if they did care?

But I guess I'm getting ahead of myself a little . . .

I dropped the shotgun between Tom and Uncle John. Then, leaving John's horse and wagon where they were, I plodded back across country to the Hauck farm.

It was pretty late by that time, or pretty early I should say. An hour or so short of dawn. I hitched up, without going to the house, and headed for town.

The livery stable door was open, the hostler snoring like a buzz saw up in the hayloft. A lantern stood burning in a tub of sand, casting a flickering light along the row of stalls. I put up the horse and buggy without hardly a sound, and the hostler went on snoring. And I went out into the dark again, the dark and the rain.

There wasn't no one on the street, of course. Even without the rain, no one would have been out at that hour. I got to the courthouse, took off my boots and sneaked upstairs to bed.

The dry-warm felt awful good after them wet clothes, and I guess I was plumb wore out. Because I went to sleep right away, instead of tossing around fifteen, twenty minutes like I usually do.

Then, just about the time my head touched the pillow it seemed like, Myra started yelling and shaking me.

'Nick! Nick Corey, you get up from there! My goodness, do you want to sleep all night and all day, too?'

'Why not?' I mumbled, hanging on to the pillows. 'Sounds like a danged good idea.'

'I said to *get up*! It's almost noon, and Rose is on the phone!'

I let her get me up, and I talked to Rose for a minute or two. I said I was sorry to hear that Tom wasn't home yet, and I'd probably get out and take a look around for him, even if I wasn't sure that the sun would stay out and it wouldn't start raining again.

'I'll prob'ly do it, Rose,' I said, 'so don't you worry none. I reckon I'll prob'ly start lookin' for him today, even if it does start raining again and I spoil my clothes like I did last night, not to mention catchin' an awful cold. Or if I don't get out today, I'll sure do it tomorrow.'

I hung up the phone and turned around.

Myra was frowning at me, tight-mouthed and disgusted-looking. She pointed to the table and told me to sit down, for pity's sake.

'Just eat your breakfast and get out of here! Start doing your job, for a change!'

'Me?' I said. 'I do my job all the time.'

'*You!* You stupid silly spineless fool! You don't do anything!'

'Well, that's my job,' I said. 'Not doing nothing, I mean. That's why for people elect me.'

She whirled around so fast her skirts spun, and went out into the kitchen. I sat down at the table. I looked at the clock and saw that it was almost twelve o'clock, practically dinner time, so I didn't eat much except some eggs and ham and grits and gravy and seven or eight biscuits, and a bitty bowl of peaches and cream.

I was having a third cup of coffee when Myra came back in. She began to snatch up the dishes, muttering to herself, and I asked her if they was something the matter.

'If they is,' I said, 'you just tell me all about it, because two heads is better than one.'

'You miserable—! Aren't you ever going to get out of here?' she yelled. 'Why are you still sitting at the table?'

'Why, I'm drinking this here coffee,' I said. 'You look real close an' you can see that I am.'

'Well – well, take it with you! Drink it somewhere else!'

'You mean you want me to leave the table?' I said.

'*Yes!* Now, go on and do it, for pity's sake!'

I said I plumb liked to be obliging, but if she studied it over she'd see it didn't make much sense for me to leave the table. 'I mean, it's almost time for dinner,' I said. 'You'll be bringin' it in any minute now, so why for should I leave when I can set right here an' be all ready to start eatin'?'

'Y-You!' Her teeth gritted together. '*You get out of here!*'

'Without no dinner?' I said. 'You mean I got to work all afternoon on an empty stomach?'

'But you just got—' She choked up, and sagged down into a chair.

I said that was fine, she should set down and rest herself up a little, and it didn't matter at all if dinner was maybe a minute or two late. And she said—

I don't know what she said. We just went on talking back and forth for a while, neither of us really listening to the other. Which didn't bother her any, since she never paid any attention to me anyhow, and to tell the truth I never actually paid a lot of attention to her, anyhow. Anyways, I couldn't have done it today even if I'd wanted to, because I was too worried about what would happen when Tom and Uncle John were found dead.

That's why I'd been pestering Myra, I guess. I didn't want to get out and face up to whatever was going to happen, so I'd start gigging at her. That was kind of a habit with me, I reckon, taking it out on her when I felt bad or bothered. More of a habit than I maybe realized.

'Where at is Lennie?' I said, picking up the conversation again. 'He don't hurry up he'll be late for dinner!'

'He's had his dinner! I mean, I fixed him a lunch before he left!'

'You mean he's outside when maybe the sun will stop shining pretty soon and it'll start raining to beat heck, and he'll probably spoil his clothes and get himself an awful cold?' I said. 'Now, that ain't takin' very good care of your brother, honey.'

Myra's face began to swell, kind of like she was blowing out her cheeks. She stared at me, her eyes popping, and god-dang if she didn't sort of tremble all over.

'Why for did Lennie go out in the daytime, anyways?' I said. 'He can't peek in no windows when it's light.'

'You!' Myra said, pushing herself up from the chair. 'Y-You—' She pointed toward the door, her hand shaking like a leaf. 'You get out of here, you hear me? GET OUT OF HERE!'

'You mean, you want me to leave?' I said. 'Well, you should've said so sooner. Maybe given me a little hint.'

I put on my hat, and told her to be sure and call me when dinner was ready. She made a wild grab for the sugar bowl, and I got on down the stairs pretty fast.

I sat down in my office. I tilted my hat over my eyes, and put my boots up on the desk. It looked to me like it was a good time to take a little nap, because people still weren't getting around much on account of the mud. But this was one day I just couldn't keep my eyes closed.

Finally, I stopped trying. There just wasn't much point to it with me so scared-worried. I figured the best thing I could do was to get things over with; get some fellas together and start the hunt for Tom. Then, whatever happened, I'd know what it was, at least, and I wouldn't have to fret myself anymore.

I got up and started for the door. The phone rang, and I went back to answer it. And just as I did, Lennie came busting in.

He was waving his arms, burbling and spitting all-the-heck over everything with excitement.

I waved him to simmer down, and spoke into the phone. 'Just a minute, Robert Lee. Lennie just came in, and it looks like he wants to tell me somethin'.'

'Never mind. I know what he wants to tell you,' Robert Lee Jefferson said, and he told me what it was. 'Now, you better get right down here and take charge.'

I said I'd do that, and I did.

It was Henry Clay Fanning, a farmer who lived a couple miles south of the Hauck place, who'd found the bodies. He'd been out cutting cordwood at the time, and he'd just pitched 'em up on top of his load and brought 'em on into town.

'Didn't waste a minute,' he said proudly, spitting snuff into the mud. 'You reckon the county'll sort of take care o' me for my trouble?'

'Well, I'm not real sure they will, Henry Clay,' I said, noticing how Uncle John's head was crushed between the wood and the wagon bed. 'After all, you was comin' to town anyways.'

'But what about that nigger?' he said. 'A white man ought to get some kind of ree-ward for handlin' a nigger.'

'Well, maybe you will,' I said. 'If not in this world, the next one.'

He went on arguing about it. Some of the people in the crowd picked up the argument, debating it back and forth between themselves. They were about evenly divided on the subject, one group claiming that Henry Clay *was* entitled to a reward, and the other saying that a white that was fool enough to bother with a nigger didn't deserve nothing but an ass-kicking.

I grabbed hold of a couple of colored fellas, and told 'em to carry Uncle John's body back to his folks. And they kind of dragged their feet, but of course they did it. Then, me and Robert Lee and one of his clerks carried Tom into Taylor's Emporium, Furniture and Undertaking.

I told Robert Lee I'd kind of like his opinion on things, and he turned on me, looking sickish. 'Can't you at least let me wash my hands?' he snapped. 'Are you in such an all-fired hurry I can't even do that?'

'Not me,' I said. 'I ain't in no more hurry than ol' Tom is, and I sure don't see him bein' in one, do you, Robert Lee? Kind of hard to tell which is the biggest, ol' Tom or the hole in him!'

We all washed up in the rear of the Emporium, Robert Lee looking awful pale and sickish. Then his clerk went on back to the hardware store, me an' Robert Lee following him maybe ten minutes later. We couldn't make it any sooner than that, because Robert Lee had to make himself another quick trip and a long visit to the wash-sink.

He held himself straight and tight-lipped as we left, still as pale as a ghost. Then, just as we stepped out the door, Henry Clay Fanning latched hold of him.

That Henry Clay was a real case, what we call a cotton-patch lawyer down here. He knew all the privileges he was entitled to – and maybe three or four million others besides – but he didn't have much sense of his obligations. None of his fourteen kids had ever been to school, because making kids go to school was interferin' with a man's constitutional rights. Four of his seven girls, all of 'em that were old enough to be, were pregnant. And he wouldn't allow no one to ask 'em how they'd got that way, because that was his legal responsibility, it was a father's job to care for his children's morals, and he didn't have to tolerate any interference.

Of course, everyone had a pretty good idea who'd gotten those girls pregnant. But under the circumstances, there wasn't any way of proving it, and with Henry Clay being kind of mean-tempered no one talked much about it.

So here he was now, exercisin' his rights again. Grabbing Robert Lee Jefferson by the arm and whirling him around.

'Now, you see here, Robert Lee,' he said. 'Maybe that doggone Nick Corey don't know the law, but you do and you know god-dang well I'm entitled to a ree-ward. I—'

'What?' Robert Lee started at him. 'What did you say?'

'County pays a ree-ward for corpses pulled out of the river, don't they? So why don't I get a bounty for finding these? I not only found 'em, I haul 'em all the way into town an' get nigger blood all over my wagon, an'—'

'Answer me, you incestuous skunk! Did you address me as Robert Lee?'

Henry Clay said sure, he called him that, and what about it, 'What you mean callin' me a—'

Robert Lee hit him in the mouth. Henry Clay sailed off the sidewalk, and landed in the mud on his back. His eyes were open, but he didn't stir. Just lay there, breathing with a snuffling sound because of his bloody nose and mouth.

Robert Lee dusted his hands, nodded to me and entered his store. I followed him back to his office.

'Now, I feel better,' he sighed, sinking down in a chair. 'I've been wanting to punch that dirty cur for years, and he finally gave me an excuse.'

I said I guessed Henry Clay didn't really know a lot about law, after all. 'If he did, he'd know that calling you by your first name would be laying a predicate for justifiable assault.'

'What?' He gave me a startled look. 'I'm not sure I understood you.'

'Nothin',' I said. 'You sure gave him a punch, Robert Lee.'

'Wasn't it a beaut? I only wish I'd broken his filthy neck.'

'Maybe you'd better be kind of careful for a while,' I said. 'Henry Clay might try to get back at you.'

Robert Lee snorted. 'He doesn't have the nerve, but I wish he did. That's one man I'd enjoy killing. Imagine him calling me by my first name!'

'Yeah,' I said, 'just imagine that!'

'Now, about this other matter, Tom and Uncle John, I don't see much point in impaneling a coroner's jury in such a clear-cut case. The facts seem obvious enough, don't you agree?'

'Well, it sure is a clear-cut case,' I said. 'I don't know as I've ever seen such a clear-cut case of killing.'

'Exactly. And everyone I've talked to has the same opinion. Of course, if Rose should insist on an inquest . . .'

'Or Uncle John's kinfolks . . .'

'Oh, now—' Robert Lee laughed. 'Let's not be ridiculous, Nick.'

'I say something funny?' I said.

'Well, uh,' said Robert Lee, sort of clearing his throat. 'Perhaps I chose the wrong word. I should have said impractical.'

I looked blank, and asked just what did he mean, anyways? He snapped back that I knew very well what he meant. 'No doctor is going to do a post mortem on a Negro. Why, you can't get a doctor to touch a live Negro, let alone a dead one.'

'I reckon you're right,' I said. 'Just in case we had to, though, and I'm just asking for information, do you suppose you could get out a court order t'make a doctor do his duty?'

'We-el' – Robert Lee leaned back and pursed his lips – 'I imagine that's something that one could do *de jure*, but not *de facto*. In other words you'd have a paradox – the legal right to do something that was factually impossible of accomplishment.'

I said I'd be god-danged, he was sure one heck of a smart man. 'I reckon my head's plumb bustin' from all these things you been tellin' me, Robbie Lee. Maybe I better run along before you give me some more information, an' it pops wide open.'

'Now, you're flattering me,' he beamed, standing up as I did, 'which reminds me that I should compliment you on your conduct in today's affair. You handled it very well, Nick.'

'Why, thank you kindly, Robert Lee,' I said. 'How does the election look to you by now, if you don't mind my asking?'

'I think you're a cinch to win, in view of the unfortunate talk about Sam Gaddis. Just keep on doing your job, like you did today.'

'Oh, I will,' I said. 'I'll keep on exactly like that.'

I left the hardware store, and sauntered back toward the courthouse, stopping now and then to talk to people, or rather to let them talk to me. Almost everyone had about the same idea about the killing as Robert Lee Jefferson. Almost everyone agreed that it was an open and shut case, with Uncle John killing Tom and then Tom, dead as he was, killing Uncle John. Or vice versa.

About the only people who didn't see it that way, or said they didn't, were some loafers. They wanted a coroner's jury impaneled, and they were ready and willin' to serve on it. But if they were that hard up for a couple of dollars, I figured they hadn't paid their poll tax, so what they thought didn't matter.

Rose had heard the news from probably two, three hundred people by the time I got back to the courthouse, and Myra said I had get out to the Hauck place right away and bring Rose into town.

'Now, please hurry, for once in your life, Nick! The poor thing is terribly upset!'

'Why for is she upset?' I said. 'You mean because Tom is dead?'

'Of course, I mean that! What else would I mean?'

'Well, I was just wonderin',' I said. 'She was terribly upset last night when she thought he might be comin' home, and now she's terribly upset because she knows he ain't. Don't seem to make much sense somehow.'

'Now, just you never mind!' Myra snapped. 'Don't you dare start arguing with me, Nick Corey! You just do what I tell you to, or *you* won't make much sense! Not that you ever did, anyway.'

I got the horse and buggy and drove out toward the Hauck farm, thinking to myself that a fella hardly got one problem settled before he had to take care of another one. Maybe I should have foreseen that Rose would be coming in and staying with Myra and me tonight, but I hadn't. I'd had too many other things on my mind. So now I was supposed to see Amy tonight – I'd just better see her if I *ever* wanted to see her again. And I was also supposed to stay at home – Rose would think it was god-danged peculiar if I didn't. And I just didn't know what the heck I was going to do.

They were a real problem, Rose and Amy. A lot bigger problem than I realized.

The farm house was all steamy and kind of smelly when Rose let me in. She apologized for it, nodding toward the black dress that was hung up over the stove.

'I had to give it a hurry-up dye job, honey. But the goddam

thing ought to be dry pretty soon. You want to come into the bedroom, and wait?'

I followed her into the bedroom and she started taking off her shoes and stockings, which was all she had on. I said, 'Looky, honey. Maybe we shouldn't do this right now.'

'Huh?' She frowned at me. 'Why the hell not?'

'Well, you know,' I said. 'You're just now officially a widow. It just don't seem decent to hop in bed with a woman when she ain't hardly been a widow an hour.'

'What the hell's the difference? You slept with me before I was a widow?'

'Well, sure,' I said. 'But everybody does things like that. You might say it was even kind of a compliment to a woman. But this way, when a woman ain't been a widow long enough to get her weeds wet, it just ain't respectful. I mean, after all, they's certain proprieties to observe, and a decent fella don't hop right on a brand-new widow any more than a decent brand-new widow lets him.'

She hesitated, studying me, but finally she nodded.

'Well, maybe you're right, Nick. Christ knows I've always done my goddam best to be respectable, in spite of that son-of-a-bitch I was married to.'

'Why sure you have,' I said. 'Don't I know that, Rose?'

'So we'll wait until tonight. After Myra goes to sleep, I mean.'

'Well,' I said. 'Well, uh—'

'And now I am going to tell you a surprise.' She gave me a hug, eyes dancing. 'It won't be long now before we can forget about Myra. You can get a divorce from the old bag – Christ knows you've got plenty of grounds – or we can just say to hell with her and leave here. Because we're going to have plenty of money, Nick. Plenty!'

'Whoa, whoa now!' I said. 'What the heck are you sayin', honey?' And she laughed, and told me how it was.

Back in the beginning, when Tom was still sugarin'-up to her, he'd taken out a ten-thousand-dollar insurance policy. Ten thousand, *double indemnity*. After a year or so, when being nice got tiresome, he'd said to hell with the policy and to hell with her. But she'd kept up the premiums herself, paying for them out of her butter and egg money. Now, since Tom had been killed instead of dying a natural death, she'd collect under the double-indemnity clause. A whole twenty thousand dollars.

'Isn't it wonderful, honey?' She hugged me again. 'And that's only part of it. This is damned good farm land, even if that son-of-a-bitch was such a no-good bastard that he never put any improvements on it. Even at a forced sale, it ought to bring ten or twelve thousand dollars, and with that much money, why—'

'Now, wait a minute,' I said. 'Not so fast, honey. We can't—'

'But we can, Nick! What the hell's to stop us?'

'You just think about it,' I said. 'Think how it would look to other people. Your husband gets killed and right away you're a rich woman. He gets killed and you profit by it plenty, and you tie up with another man before his body's hardly cold. You don't think that folks would wonder about that a little! You don't think they might get some alarmin' ideas about her and this other man and her husband's death?'

'We-el . . .' Rose nodded. 'I suppose you're right, Nick. How long do you think we'll have to wait before it will be safe?'

'I'd say a year or two, anyways,' I said. 'Prob'ly two years would be best.'

Rose said she didn't think two years would be best. Not for her it wasn't. One year was going to be a goddamned plenty to wait, and she wasn't sure she'd even wait that long.

'But we got to! My gosh, honey,' I said. 'We can't take no chances, right when we've got everything the way we want it. That wouldn't make no sense, now would it?'

'Everything isn't the way *I* want it! Not by a hell of a long shot!'

'But looky, looky, honey,' I said. 'You just agreed that we had to be god-danged careful, and now you—'

'Oh, all right,' Rose laughed, kind of pouting. 'I'll try to be sensible, Nick. But don't you forget I've got my brand on you. Don't you forget it for a minute!'

'Why, honey,' I said. 'What a thing to say! Why for would I want another woman when I've got you?'

'I mean it, Nick! I mean every word of it!'

I said sure, I knew she did, so what was she carryin' on about? She untensed a little, and patted me on the cheek.

'I'm sorry, honey. We'll see each other tonight, hmmm? You know, after Myra's gone to sleep.'

'I don't see no reason why not,' I said, wishing to gosh I could see a reason.

'Mmm! I can hardly wait!' She kissed me and jumped up. 'I wonder if that goddam dress is dry yet.'

It was dry. Probably a heck of a lot dryer than I was, what with all the sweating I was doing. I thought to myself, Nick Corey, how in the good gosh-dang do you get in these god-dang messes? You got to be with Rose tonight; you just don't dare not to be with her. And you got to be with Amy Mason tonight. Anyway, you're sure aching to be with Amy, even if you don't have to be. So—

But I did have to be.

I just didn't know it yet.

16

Myra was waiting for us at the head of the stairs when me and Rose arrived, and the two of 'em practically fell into each other's arms. Myra said, you poor, poor dear, and Rose said, oh, what would I ever do without you, Myra, and then they both busted out bawling.

Myra made the most noise, of course, even though it was more Rose's place to do it, and she'd been practising all the way into town. There just wasn't no one that could beat Myra when it came to noisemaking. She started to steer Rose into her bedroom, her eyes on Rose instead of where she was going, and she bumped spang into Lennie. She whirled and gave him a slap that almost made *me* hurt. Then she hit him again because he yelled.

'Now, you shut up!' she warned him. 'Just shut up and behave yourself. Poor Rose has enough trouble without putting up with your racket!'

Lennie clenched his teeth to keep from bawling; I almost felt kind of sorry for him. Fact is, I felt real sorry for him, but right while I was doing it, I felt something else. Because that's the way I am, I guess. I start feeling sorry for people, like Rose, for example, or even Myra or Uncle John or, well, lots of folks, and the way it eventually works out is it'd be a lot better if I hadn't felt sorry for them. Better for them, I mean. And I guess that's natural enough, you know? Because when you're sorry for someone, you want to help them, and when it sinks in on you that you can't, that there's too god-danged many of them, that everywhere you look there's someone, millions of someones, and you're only one man an' no one else cares an' – an'—

We were having an oven supper that night, which was a good thing since Myra was so long in the bedroom with Rose. Finally, they came out, and I patted Rose on the shoulder and told her she'd have to be brave. She rested her head against my chest for a moment, like she just couldn't help herself, and I gave her another pat.

'Now, that's right, Nick,' Myra said. 'You just take care of Rose, and I'll get supper on.'

'I'll sure do that,' I said, 'me an' Lennie'll both take care of her, won't we, Lennie?'

Lennie scowled, blaming Rose naturally because Myra had hit him. Myra gave him a frown and told him he'd better watch his step. Then she went into the kitchen to take up supper.

It was god-danged good, being a company meal. Rose remembered to bust into tears now and then, and say that she just couldn't eat a bite. But she couldn't have put away much more without letting out her dress.

Myra filled up our coffee cups, and brought in dessert, two kinds of pie and a chocolate cake. Rose had some of each, shedding a few tears at intervals to show that she was just forcin' herself.

We finished eating. Rose got up to help, but of course, Myra wouldn't hear of it.

'No, sir, no, siree! You sit right down there on the settee, and rest your poor dear self!'

'But it's not fair to leave you with all the work, Myra, darling,' Rose said. 'I could at least do—'

'Nothing, absolutely nothing!' Myra shooed her away. 'You're going to sit down, that's what you're going to do. Nick, you entertain Rose while I'm busy.'

'Why, sure,' I said. 'Nothin' I'd enjoy more than entertainin' Rose!'

Rose had to bite her lip to keep from laughin'. We went over to the settee and sat down, and Myra gathered up an armful of dishes and started for the kitchen.

Lennie was lolling on a chair with his eyes closed. But I knew they weren't closed tight. That was a trick of his, pretending to be asleep, and I guess he must have liked it real well because this was about the umpteenth time he'd tried to pull it on me.

I whispered to Rose, 'How about a little kiss, honey?'

Rose shot a quick look at Lennie and the kitchen door, and said, 'Let's have a big one.' And we had a big one.

And Lennie's eyes and mouth flew open at the same time, and he let out a yell. 'My-ra! Myra, come quick, Myra!'

There was a heck of a clatter as Myra dropped something in the kitchen. A stack of dishes, it sounded like. She ran in, scared out of her wits, looking like she expected the house to be on fire.

'What? What, what?' she said. 'What's going on? What's the matter, Lennie?'

'They was huggin' and kissin', Myra!' Lennie pointed at Rose and me. 'I seen 'em, huggin' and kissin'.'

'Why, Lennie,' I said. 'How can you say such a awful thing?'

'You was too! I seen you!'

'Now, you know that ain't so!' I said. 'You know god-danged good an' well what happened.'

'Just what did happen?' Myra said, looking kind of uncertainly from Rose to me. 'I'm – I'm sure there must be a, uh, mistake, but—'

Rose started crying again, burying her face in her hands. She got up, saying she was going home because she just couldn't stay another minute in a place where people said such awful things about her.

Myra put out a hand to stop her, and said, 'Nick, will you kindly tell me what this is all about?'

'They was huggin' and kissin', that's what!' Lennie yelled. 'I seen 'em!'

'Hush, hush, Lennie! Nick?'

'T'heck with it,' I said, sounding mad. 'You can believe any god-danged thing you want to. I tell you this, though, this is the last god-danged time I try to comfort anyone when they're feelin' bad!'

'But . . . oh,' said Myra. 'You mean that . . .?'

'I mean that Rose got to feelin' real bad again,' I said. 'She started cryin' and I told her to just lean against me until she felt better, and I sort of patted her on the shoulder like any decent fella would. Why, god-dang it!' I said, 'I did the same god-dang thing a while ago when you were right here in the room, and you said that was fine, I should take care of her! And god-dang, look how you're actin' now!'

'Please, Nick,' Myra was all flustered and red. 'I never for a moment thought that, uh—'

'It's all my fault,' Rose said, drawing herself up real dignified. 'I guess I can't blame you for thinking such terrible things about me, Myra, but you should have known that I'd never, never do anything to hurt my very best friend.'

'But I do know it! I never had any such thoughts, Rose, darling!' Myra was practically bawling herself. 'I'd never doubt you for a moment, dear.'

'They're story-tellin', Myra!' Lennie yelled. 'I seen 'em huggin' and kissin'.'

Myra slapped him. She pointed to the door of his room, chasing him toward it with a couple more hard slaps. 'Now, you get in there! Get right in there and don't let me see you again tonight!'

'But I seen—'

Myra gave him a crack that practically knocked him off his feet. He went stumbling into his bedroom, blubbering and spitting, and she slammed the door on him.

'I'm terribly, terribly sorry, Rose, darling,' Myra turned back around again. 'I – *Rose!* You take that hat right back off, because you're not moving a step out of here!'

'I th-think I'd better go home,' Rose wept, but she didn't sound real determined. 'I'd be too embarrassed to stay after this.'

'But you mustn't be, dear! There's absolutely no need to be. Why—'

'But she does,' I cut in, 'an' I don't blame her a god-dang bit! I feel the same way myself. Why, god-dang it, the way I feel right now I get sort of self-conscious even bein' in the same room with Rose!'

'Well, why don't you get out of the same room then?' Myra snapped. 'My goodness, get out and take a walk or something! No sense in you acting the fool, just because poor Lennie did.'

'All right, I will get out,' I said. 'That god-danged Lennie starts all the trouble, and I get drove out of my own house. So don't you be surprised if I don't hurry back!'

'I'll be pleasantly surprised if you don't. I'm sure neither Rose nor I will miss you, will we, Rose?'

'Well—' Rose bit her lip. 'I hate to feel responsible for—'

'Now, don't you trouble yourself another minute, darling. You just come out in the kitchen with me, and we'll have a nice cup of coffee.'

Rose went with her, looking just a wee bit disappointed, naturally. At the kitchen door, she glanced back at me quickly, and I shrugged and spread my hands and looked sort of mournful. As if to say, you know, that it was too doggoned bad, but it was just one of those things, and what could you do about it? And she nodded, letting me know that she understood.

I got a pole and fishing line from under my bed. I came back out of the bedroom and called to Myra, asking her if she could pack me up a lunch because I was going fishing. And I guess you know what she told me. So I left.

There weren't many people on the street that late at night,

almost nine o'clock, but practically everybody that was up asked me if I was going fishing. I said, why, no, I wasn't, and where did they ever get an idea like that?

'Well, how come you're carryin' a fish pole and line, then?' this one fella said. 'How come you're doin' that if you ain't goin' fishin'.'

'Oh, I got that to scratch my butt with,' I said. 'Just in case I'm up a tree somewheres, an' I can't reach myself from the ground.'

'But, looky here now—' He hesitated, frowning. 'That don't make no sense.'

'How come it don't?' I said. 'Why, practically everyone I know does the same thing. You mean to say you never took a fishing pole with you to scratch your butt with, in case you was up a tree an' couldn't reach yourself from the ground? Why, god-dang it, ain't you behind the times!'

He said, well, sure, he always did the same thing himself. Fact is, he was the first fella to think of the idea. 'All I meant was that you shouldn't have no hook an' line on it. I mean, that part don't make sense.'

'Why, shore it does,' I said. 'That's to pull up the back-flap of your drawers after you're through scratchin'. God-dang,' I said, 'it looks to me like you're really behind the times, fella. You don't watch out, the world will plumb pass you by before you know it!'

He scuffed his feet, looking ashamed of himself. I went on down the street toward the river.

I told one fella that, no, I wasn't going fishing, I was going to fasten on to a sky-hook and swing myself t' the other side of the river. I told another fella that, no, I wasn't going fishing, the county was putting a bounty on flying turds and I was going to try to hook onto some, in case they cleaned out the crappers when the train went by. I told another fella—

Well, never mind. It don't make no more difference than it made sense.

I got to the river. I waited a while, and then I began moving up the bank until I was about on a line with Amy Mason's house. Then, I started cutting back toward town again, dodging any house with lights in it and taking cover whenever I could. And finally I got to where I was going.

Amy let me in the back door. It was dark, and she took my hand and led me back to the bedroom. She flung off her nightgown there, grabbed me and held me for a minute, her lips moving over my face. She began to whisper, wild crazy things, sweet wild crazy things. And her hands fumbled with my clothes, and I thought to myself, god-danged, there just never was no one like Amy! There just ain't no one like her! And . . .

And I was right.

She made me know I was.

Then, we were lying side by side, holding hands. Breathing together, our hearts beating together. Somehow, there was perfume in the air, although I knew Amy never wore none; and somehow you could hear violins playin', so sweet and so soft, playing a song that never was. It was like there wasn't any yesterday, like there'd been no time before this, and I wondered why it should ever be any other way.

'Amy,' I said, and she rolled her head to look at me. 'Let's get away from this town, honey, let's us run away together.'

She was silent for a moment, seeming to think the idea over. Then she said I couldn't think very much of her or I wouldn't make such a suggestion.

'You're a married man. I'm afraid you might have a great deal of trouble in getting unmarried. What does that make me, the woman who runs away with you?'

'Well, looky, honey,' I said. 'This sure ain't satisfactory, the way we're doin' now. We sure can't go on like this, can we?'

'Do we have a choice?' Her shoulders moved in a shrug. 'Now if you had money – you don't, do you, dear? No, I thought not – you might be able to make a settlement with your wife, and we could leave town. But in the absence of money . . .'

'Well, uh, about that now . . .' I cleared my throat. 'I reckon they's a lot of fellas that'd be too proud to accept money from a woman. But the way I look at it—'

'I don't have it, Nick, popular opinion to the contrary notwithstanding. I own a number of income properties, and the rentals enable me to live quite well by Pottsville standards. But they'd bring very little at a sale. Certainly not enough to support two people for the rest of their lives, let alone assuage the wounded feelings of a wife like yours.'

I hardly knew what to say to that. Maybe, well, maybe my feelings was kind of hurt. Because I knew just about as much about the property she owned as she did, and I knew she was a lot better off than she pretended.

She just didn't want to get things squared up and go off with me. Or just run away with me like any woman should if she was really in love with a fella. But it was her money, so what the heck could I do about it?

Amy picked up my hand and put it on one of her breasts. She squeezed it, trying to press it into her flesh, but I didn't help her none, and finally she pushed it away.

'All right, Nick,' she said. 'I'll tell you the real reason I won't go away with you.'

I said to never mind, I wouldn't want to trouble her none, and she snapped for me not to dare to be rude to her. 'Don't you dare, Nicholas Corey! I love you – at least, it seems to be love to me – and because I do, I'm willing to accept something that I never thought I could accept. But don't you be rude to me, or I might change. I might cease to love a man who I know is a murderer!'

17

didn't say anything for quite a spell; just lay still where I was wondering where that violin music had gone to and why I couldn't smell the perfume no more.

Finally, I said, 'Just what are you talking about, Amy?' And I was just a little relieved when she told me, just a little, because it could have been a lot worse.

'I'm talking about those two men you killed. Those, well, pimps is the word, I believe.'

'Pimps?' I said. 'What pimps?'

'Stop it, Nick. My reference is to a certain night when you and I returned to Pottsville on the same train. Yes, I know you didn't see me, but I was on it. I was curious as to why you'd be going to the river at that time of night, dressed in your very best clothes, so I followed you . . .'

'Now listen,' I said. 'You couldn't've followed me wherever I went. It was doggoned dark that night that—'

'It was very dark for you, Nick. For a man who's never been able to see well at night. But I don't suffer from that handicap. I followed you quite easily, and I saw you quite clearly when you killed those two men.'

Well . . .

At least it was better than her knowing I'd killed the other two. It didn't tie me up with Rose in a way that I couldn't very well get out of. Which Amy would have known was the case if she knew I'd killed Tom Hauck. And which was still the case even if Amy didn't know about it.

For a minute or two, I almost wished I was running off with Rose and thirty thousand dollars plus, and t'heck with Amy. But my thinking that was just almost and I didn't even almost it very long. Rose just naturally took too much out of a fella, she was too demandin' and possessive, and she didn't have much of anything to give him back. She was one heck of a lot of woman, but when you'd said that you'd said it all. A lot of woman but a god-danged flighty one. A woman who was apt to lose her head just when she needed it most, like she had with Uncle John.

I rolled over and took Amy into my arms. She swam up against me for a moment, pressing every soft warm inch of herself again me, and then she kind of moaned and pulled away.

'Why did you do it, Nick? I told you I'd accepted it, and I have, but – why, darling? Make me understand why! I never thought you could kill anyone.'

'I never thought I could neither,' I said. 'And I can't rightly say why I did it. They were just one more god-dang thing I didn't like, that I particularly didn't like. I'd been letting them go, like I let so many things go, and finally I thought, well, I didn't have to. There were a lot of things, most things, that I couldn't do nothing about. But I *could* do something about them, an' finally . . . finally I did something.'

Amy stared at me, a little frown working up on her face. I gave her a pat on the bottom, and kissed her again.

'T'tell the truth, honey,' I went on, 'I really felt like I was doing the right thing for them fellas. They weren't no good to themselves nor nobody else and they must've known it, like anyone would know a thing like that. So I was doing 'em a pure kindness by fixing it so they wouldn't have to go on livin'.'

'I see,' Amy said. 'I see. And do you also feel you'd be doing Ken Lacey a pure kindness if you kept him from going on living?'

'Him especially,' I said. 'A fella that mocks his friends, that hurts people just because he's able to hurt 'em – Ken Lacey!' I said. 'What do you know about him?'

'Only one thing, Nick. All I know is that you somehow seem to have arranged things so that Sheriff Lacey will be blamed for the two murders that you committed.'

I swallowed, and said I just didn't know how she figured that. 'It sure ain't my fault if Ken comes down here an' gets drunk, and pops off all over town about what a tough fella he is. I figure that if a fella wants to get all the glory out of braggin', he has to take the blame along with it.'

'I don't figure that way, Nick. I won't allow you to do it.'

'But, looky,' I said. 'Why not, Amy? What's Ken to you, anyways?'

'He's a man who may be falsely convicted of murder.'

'But – but I just don't understand,' I said. 'If you don't mind about me killin' them two pimps, why . . .'

'You haven't been listening, Nick. I mind about them very much. But I had no way of knowing that you were going to kill them. In the case of Sheriff Lacey, I do know your plans, and if I allowed you to carry them out I'd be as guilty as you are.'

'But' – I hesitated – 'what if I just can't help myself, Amy? What if it's him or me?'

'Then, I'd be very sorry, Nick. It would have to be you. But that circumstance isn't likely to arise, is it? There's no way you can be incriminated?'

'Well, no,' I said. 'I can't think of none offhand. For that matter, there's a good chance them bodies will never be found.'

'Well, then?'

'Well . . . god-dang it, Amy, it'd be a lot better to let things go like I planned!' I said. 'A whole lot better. Why, if you knew that god-danged Ken Lacey like I do, some of the mean things he's done—'

'No, Nick. Absolutely, no.'

'But, doggone it—!'

'No.'

'Now, you looky here, Amy,' I said. 'It just don't look to me like you're in any position to be givin' orders. You got guilty knowledge, like they say in the courts. You know I killed those fellas an' you didn't say nothin' about it, so if you try to do it later you're incriminatin' yourself.'

'I know that,' Amy nodded evenly. 'But I'd still do it, Nick. I'm sure you know I would.'

'But—'

But I *did* know she'd do it, even if it got her hanged. So there just wasn't anything more to say on the subject.

I looked at her, with her hair spilled out on the pillows and the warmth of her body warming mine. And I thought, god-dang, if this ain't a heck of a way to be in bed with a pretty woman. The two of you arguing about murder, and threatening each other, when you're supposed to be in love and you could be doing something pretty nice. And then I thought, well, maybe it ain't so strange after all. Maybe it's like this with most people, everyone doing pretty much the same thing except in a different way. And all the time they're holding heaven in their hands.

'I'm sorry, honey,' I said. 'O' course, I'll do whatever you want. I wouldn't never want to do nothing else.'

'And I'm sorry, too, darling.' She brushed my mouth with a kiss. 'And I'll do what you want. As soon as things here are a little more settled, I'll go away with you.'

'Fine. That's just fine, honey,' I said.

'I want to very much, dear, and I will. Just as soon as we can be sure that there are no loose ends here.'

I said again that that was just fine, wondering what I was going to do about a great big loose end like Rose Hauck. Then I thought, well, I'd just have to face that problem when I came to it. And I put everything out of my mind but Amy, and I reckon she put everything out of her mind but me. And it was like it was before, only more so.

It was like nothing that ever was. Only more so.

Then, again we were layin' there side by side. Breathing together, hearts beating together. And suddenly Amy tore her hand out of mine, and sat up.

'Nick! What's that?'

'What? What's what?'

I looked to the window where she was pointing, at the drawn shade with its rim of flickering light.

Then, I jumped up and ran to the window, and tilted the shade back. And I guess I must have groaned out loud.

'God-dang,' I said. 'God-dang it to heck, anyway!'

'Nick, what is it, darling?'

'Colored town. It's on fire.'

I guess I should have known it might happen. Because Tom Hauck *was* a white man, whatever else you said about him, and it looked like a colored fella had killed him. So some idjit would get the notion that 'the niggers got to be taught a lesson,' and he'd spread the word to other idjits. And pretty soon there'd be trouble.

I got dressed with Amy watchin' me worriedly. She asked me what I was going to do, and I said I didn't know, but I was sure going to have to do something. Because a thing like this, a sheriff bein' off fishing when trouble broke, was just the kind of thing that could lose an election.

'But, Nick . . . that doesn't matter now, does it? As long as we're going away together?'

'When?' I jerked on my boots. 'You can't name no definite date, can you?'

'Well—' She bit her lip. 'I see what you mean, dear.'

'Might be a year or two,' I said. 'But even if it was only six months, I better be in office. Makes it a lot easier to wrap up any of them loose ends you mentioned than it would if I was just an ordinary citizen.'

I finished dressing, and she let me out the back door.

I went back the way I'd come, down to the river, then up the river bank. And of course I didn't keep my fishing pole with me.

I came up on the far side of the Negro section, dirtyin' myself with some charcoal from the fire. Then, I mingled in with the crowd, beating at the flames with a wet toesack that someone had dropped.

Actually, there wasn't a whole lot of damage; maybe a total of six or seven burned shacks. What with the recent rain and no wind, the fire was slow in starting and it didn't have a chance to spread far before it was discovered.

I started telling some colored folks what to do, working right along with them. Then, I stood back for a minute, wiping the sweat from my eyes, and someone tapped me on the shoulder.

It was Robert Lee Jefferson, and he looked about as stern as I'd ever seen him.

'God-dang, ain't this something, Robert Lee?' I said. 'No telling what might have happened if I hadn't been right here Johnny-on-the-spot when the fire broke out.'

'Come along,' he said.

'Why, thanks, Robert Lee,' I said, 'but I don't rightly think I can. This fire—'

'The fire is fully under control. It was under control long before you got here. Now, come along.'

I climbed into his carriage with him. We drove to his store, and there were other carriages and buggies and horses tied up outside, and there were maybe a half a dozen men waiting on the sidewalk. Important citizens like Mr Dinwiddie, the bank president, and Zeke Carlton, who owned the cotton gin, and Stonewall Jackson Smith, the school superintendent, and Samuel Houston Taylor, who owned Taylor's Emporium, Furniture and Undertaking.

We all went inside. We sat down in Robert Lee's office, or I should say, everybody but me sat down. Because there just wasn't no place for me to sit.

Zeke Carlton started the meeting by slamming his fists down on the desk and asking just what the hell kind of county were we running. 'Do you know what can come of a thing like this tonight, Nick? Do you know what happens when a bunch of poor helpless niggers get burned out?'

'I got a pretty good idea,' I said. 'All the colored folks get scared, and maybe they ain't around when it comes cotton-pickin' time.'

'You're tootin' well right, they're not! Scarin' them god-dam poor niggers could cost us all a pisspot full of money!'

'Your wife said you'd gone fishing tonight,' Robert Lee Jefferson said. 'At just what point on the river were you when the fire broke out?'

'I didn't go fishing,' I said.

'Now, Corey,' Stonewall Jackson Smith said firmly. 'I saw you heading toward the river myself with a fishing pole and line. I'd say that was pretty conclusive evidence that you did go fishing.'

'Well, now, I just don't think I can agree with you,' I said. 'I wouldn't say you was wrong, but I sure wouldn't say you was right, neither.'

'Oh, cut it out, Nick!' snapped Samuel Houston Taylor. 'We—'

'Take t'other night, now,' I went on, 'I seen a certain fella crawlin' into an empty freight car with a certain high school teacher. But I don't think that's conclusive evidence they was shipping themselves somewhere.'

Stonewall Jackson turned fiery red. The others looked at him, kind of narrow-eyed, like they was sizing him up for the first time, and Mr Dinwiddie, the bank president, turned to me. He was friendlier than the other fellas. He'd stayed pretty friendly toward me ever since the time I'd pulled him out of the privy.

'Just where were you and what were you doing there tonight, Sheriff?' he said. 'I'm sure we'll all be glad to accept your explanation.'

'Not me, by God!' said Zeke Carlton. 'I—'

'Quiet, Zeke,' Mr Dinwiddie motioned to him. 'Go on, Sheriff.'

'Well, we'll start right at the beginning of tonight,' I said. 'I figured someone might try to start somethin' with the colored folks, so I got out a pole an' line and pretended to go fishing. The river runs right in back of colored town, you know, an'—'

'Yeah, hell, we know where it runs!' Samuel Houston Taylor scowled. 'What we want to know is why you weren't there to prevent the fire?'

'Because I had to make a little detour,' I said. 'I seen a fella sneakin' away from someone's house, and I thought maybe he'd pulled something crooked. It looked like something I ought to investigate, anyways, just to make sure. So I went up to this house, and I was about to knock when I decided it wasn't necessary and it might be kind of embarrassin'. Because I could see this housewife inside, and it was plain to see, as happy as she looked, that there hadn't been no trouble. Aside from which she didn't have hardly no clothes on.'

It was just a shot in the dark, of course. Sort of a double shot. I figured that with this many Pottsville citizens involved, someone was just about bound to be two-timin' his wife, or someone's wife was two-timin' him. Or else he was god-dang suspicious that she was.

Anyways, it sure looked like my shot hit home, because it was the dangest funniest thing you ever seen, the way they acted. All of 'em – or most of 'em, I should say – glaring at each other and trying to keep their heads ducked at the same time. All of 'em accused and accusing.

Mr Dinwiddie started to ask just whose house I was referring to. But the others gave him a look that shut him up fast.

Robert Lee cleared his throat, and said for me to go on with my story.

'We can assume that you eventually reached the river, and you were there when the fire started. Then, what happened?

What were you doing all the time that the rest of us were fighting the blaze?'

'I was trying to catch the fellas that started it,' I said. 'They came crashing down through the underbrush afterward, trying to get away, and I hollered for 'em to halt, they was under arrest, but it didn't do no good. They kept on running, and I chased 'em, yelling for them to stop or I'd shoot. But I reckon they knew I wouldn't, knew I wouldn't dare to, because they all got away.'

Robert Lee wet his lips, hesitating. 'Did you see who they were, Nick?'

'Well, let's put it this way,' I said. 'It don't make much difference whether I know who they were or not. As long as I didn't catch 'em, their names ain't important and it would just cause hard feelin's to say who they was.'

'But, Sheriff,' Mr Dinwiddie said. 'I don't see, uh—' He broke off, seeing the look that Zeke Carlton gave him. Seeing the looks of the others, his most important depositors.

Because I'd fired another shot in the dark, and it had hit even closer on target than the first one.

With a couple of exceptions, there wasn't a man there that didn't have a grown or a semi-grown son. And there wasn't a one of them younguns that was worth the powder it'd take to blow their nose. They loafed around town, puttin' up a half-way pretence of working for their daddies. Whoring and drinking and thinking up meanness. Any troubles that broke out, you could bet that either one of 'em or all of 'em was mixed up in it.

The meeting broke up, hardly anyone nodding to me as they left.

I followed Robert Lee out to the walk and we stood talking together for a minute.

'I'm afraid you haven't made yourself any friends tonight, Nick,' he told me. 'You'll really have to buckle down and work from now on, if you want to stay in office.'

'Work?' I scratched my head. 'What at?'

'At your job, naturally! What else?' he said, and then his eyes shifted as I stared at him. 'All right, perhaps you did have to compromise tonight. Perhaps you'll have to again. But one or two exceptional cases don't justify your doing nothing at all to enforce the law.'

'Well, I'll tell you about that, Robert Lee,' I said. 'Practically every fella that breaks the law has a danged good reason, to his own way of thinking, which makes every case exceptional, not just one or two. Take you, for example. A lot of fellas might think you was guilty of assault and battery when you punched Henry Clay Fanning in—'

'I'll ask you just one question,' Robert Lee cut in. 'Are you or aren't you going to start enforcing the law?'

'Sure I am,' I said. 'I sure ain't going to do nothing else but.'

'Good, I'm relieved to hear it.'

'Yes, sir,' I said. 'I'm really going to start cracking down. Anyone that breaks a law from now on is goin' to have to deal with me. Providing, o' course, that he's either colored or some poor white trash that can't pay his poll tax.'

'That's a pretty cynical statement, Nick!'

'Cynical?' I said. 'Aw, now, Robert Lee. What for have I got to be cynical about?'

18

The fire was on late Friday night, and it was almost dawn Saturday before I got home. I scrubbed myself up, and put on some clean clothes. Then I went out into the kitchen, and started to fix breakfast.

Myra came out fuming and fussing, asking me what in the world I was up to. I told her about the fire and how people were criticizin' me, and she shut up fast. Because she didn't want to be an ex-sheriff's wife any more than I wanted to be an ex-sheriff, and she knew I was going to have to do some humpin' or we might be.

She finished cooking breakfast for me. I ate and went downtown.

It being Saturday, all the stores were open extra early, and any farmers that weren't already in town were on their way in. They stood around on the sidewalks, their black cloth hats brushed and clean-looking, their Sunday shirts fairly clean, and their overalls ranging from middling-dirty to downright filthy.

Their wives wore starched-stiff sunbonnets and Mother Hubbards made out of calico or gingham. Their kids' clothes – except the kids that were old enough for hand-me-downs – were made out of meal sacks, with the faded labels still showing on some of 'em. Men and women, and practically every boy and girl over twelve, were chewing and spitting snuff. The men and boys poured the snuff down inside their lower lip. The women and girls used snuff-sticks, frayed twigs that they dipped in their snuff cans and then put in the corners of their mouths.

I moved around among the men, shakin' hands and slapping backs and telling 'em to just come and see me any time they had a problem. I told all the women that Myra had been askin' about 'em and that they just had to come and see her sometime. And I patted the kids on the head, if their heads weren't too high up, and gave them pennies and nickels, depending on how tall they were.

Naturally, I was busy with the townspeople too, doing my dangdest to make friends or to get back any I'd lost. But I couldn't be sure I did any better with them than I did with the farmers, and I couldn't be sure I did any good with the farmers.

Oh, almost everyone was pleasant, and no one was what you'd call downright unfriendly. But too many of 'em were cautious, kind of cagey when I hinted around at the subject of voting. And if there's one thing I know it's this: a fella that's going to vote for you don't lose much time in declaring himself.

I tried to run a tally in my mind, and it looked to me like the best I could hope for was a near-draw with Sam Gaddis. That was the best, despite all the dirty talk that was going on about him. And if he was that strong now, in spite of the talk, how could I be sure he wouldn't be even stronger in the run-off?

I ate some crackers and cheese for lunch, passing them around amongst the fellas I was talking to.

About two o'clock. I had to go out to the cemetery for Tom Hauck's buryin', but a passel of other folks went, too, by way of amusin' themselves, so you couldn't really say it was a waste of time.

I worked through the supper hour, eating some crackers and sardines and passing them around amongest the fellas I was talking to.

Finally, it got too late to work any longer. But by then, I was so keyed up from talking, so restless and high-strung that my nerves seemed to be standing on end. So instead of going home, I sneaked over to Amy Mason's house.

We went back into the bedroom. She held me off for a minute, kind of cold and peevish-actin', and then she seemed to change her mood suddenly. And we went to bed.

It happened pretty fast, considering how wore out I was. But afterwards my eyes drifted shut, and I seemed to sink down into a deep dark pit, and—

'Wake up!' Amy was shaking me. 'Wake up, I said!'

I said, 'Huh, whassa matter, honey?' And Amy said again that I was to wake up.

'Is that how little I mean to you? That you can fall asleep like a hog in a wallow with my arms around you? Or were you saving yourself for your precious Rose Hauck?'

'Huh? What?' I said. 'For gosh sake, Amy—'

'Rose is staying at your place, is she not?'

'Well, sure,' I said. 'But just on account of her husband's death and buryin'. She—'

'And why didn't you tell me she was staying there? Why did I have to find it out for myself?'

'But, looky,' I said. 'Why the heck should I tell you? What's it got to do with us? Anyways, you already knew all about me an' Rose, an' it didn't seem to bother you none.'

She stared at me, her eyes sparkling with anger, and suddenly turned her back to me. Then, just as I was about to put my arm around her, she turned and faced me again.

'Just what do I already know about you and Rose? Tell me!'

'Aw, now, honey,' I said. 'I—'

'Answer me! Just what do I know about you? I want to know!'

I said I'd just made a slip of the tongue, and there wasn't anything to tell her about Rose and me. Because of course, she didn't want to know about us. No woman that sleeps with a man wants to know that another woman is doin' it, too.

'I was just referrin' to the other night,' I said. 'You know, when you was teasin' me about Rose, and I told you there wasn't nothing between us. That's all I meant when I said you already knew all about us.'

'Well—' She was anxious to believe me. 'You're sure?'

'O' course, I'm sure,' I said. 'Why, my gosh, ain't we the same as engaged to get married? Ain't we goin' to go away together just as soon as we figure out what to do about my wife an' we're sure there ain't any kickbacks from them two pimps I killed? That's right, ain't it, so why would I be fooling around with another woman?'

She smiled, her lips kind of trembly. She kissed me, and snuggled up in my arms.

'Nick ... don't see her anymore. After she's gone home, I mean.'

'Well, I sure don't want to,' I said. 'I sure don't aim to, anyways. I sure won't see her, Amy, unless I just can't noways get out of it.'

'Yes? And just what is that supposed to mean?'

'I mean, she's Myra's friend,' I said. 'Even before Tom got himself killed, Myra was always after me to give Rose some help, an' I felt sorry for her so I usually did. So it'll look awful funny if I stop all of a sudden, without even waitin' until she can hire a farm hand.'

Amy was silent for a moment, thinking things over. Then her head moved in a little nod.

'All right, Nick. I suppose you will have to see her – one more time.'

'Well, I'm not sure that'll be enough,' I said. 'I mean, it prob'ly will, but—'

'One more time, Nick. Just to tell her that she'd better employ some help because you won't be seeing her again. No,' – she put her hand over my mouth as I started to speak – 'that's it, Nick. Just once more, and never again. If you want me, that is. If you want to keep me from being very, very angry with you.'

I said, all right, that's the way it would be. There just wasn't much else I could say. But what I was thinking was that Rose was going to have something to say about this, and I could get in just as much trouble by not heeding her as I could Amy.

Amy just wasn't giving me a chance, god-dang it! I was just as anxious to be shet of Rose as she was to have me. But it would take time and if I didn't have the time, if I could only see Rose once more . . .

'Nick, darling . . . I'm still here.'

I said, 'Yeah, danged if you ain't.' And I hugged her close and kissed and petted her, putting a lot of enthusiasm into it. But I tell you frankly, I didn't feel much. And it wasn't just because I was so tired I could hardly lift a finger.

I'd been almost on the point of hitting on a plan, something that would not only take care of Rose without me seeing her more than once, but would take care of Myra and Lennie at the same time. And then Amy had spoke up, and the pieces of a plan had scattered every which way. And I knew I was going to have a heck of a time putting 'em together again, if I ever was able to.

'Nick!' – she was beginning to sound cross again – 'you're not going to sleep again, are you?'

'Me?' I said. 'Me go to sleep around a pretty thing like you? Now, what do you think?'

She let me out the door, so drowsy herself she could barely keep her eyes open. I sneaked back across town, and believe me, sneakin' is the word, because I was plumb wrung dry an' there wasn't enough juice left in me to wet a whistle.

I got to the courthouse, and slipped off my boots at the foot of the stairs. I sneaked up the stairs and got to my room, and got out of my clothes. Then, I slid into bed, careful as I could to keep the springs from squeaking. And I sighed and thought Oh, Lord, how long, god-dang it? One cross is bad enough, but I hadn't ought to carry a whole god-dang lumberyard around with me!

Rose grabbed me. She swarmed all over me, and it was like her body was on fire.

'Goddam! What the hell took you so long, Nick?'

I tried to keep from groaning. I said, 'Look, Rose we can't do this, honey. It's already Sunday morning.'

'Crap on Sunday morning!' she said. 'Who gives a damn what day it is?'

'But – but this ain't nice,' I said. 'It just ain't nice to fornicate on Sunday morning. Now, you just think about it, an' you'll see I'm right.'

Rose said she didn't want to think about it, she just wanted to do it. 'Come on, dammit!' she panted. 'Come on! I'll show you whether it's nice or not!'

Well, I just couldn't, you know. At least, I thought I couldn't. And I guess the only way I managed to was because the good Lord gave me strength. He seen I was in a heck of a spot, like He naturally would, because if He'd noticed something like a sparrow fallin', He'd just about have to see the predicament I was in.

So He gave me strength, I reckon. Which – an' I don't mean to sound ungrateful – was about the *least* He could do.

19

Rose went to church with Myra and me, Lennie staying at home because he didn't always behave too well in crowds. After the services, Rose and Myra went on home to get dinner ready, and I hung around to do a little handshakin' and baby-pattin' and back slappin'.

Sam Gaddis was doing the same thing, a gray haired middle-aged fella with a dignified look about him. The minister had given him a kind of indirect boost in his sermon, which was about casting stones and judge not lest ye be judged, and now he seemed to be getting a better reception than I was. People would turn their heads to look at him, while they were shaking hands with me. I'd slap 'em on the back and they'd sort of take it as a shove toward Sam. And there was one woman that yanked her baby away just as I was about to kiss it, so that I danged near kissed my own belt buckle.

It looked to me like a case of, if you can't lick 'em join 'em, so I eased my way through the crowd and grabbed Sam by the hand.

'I want you to know I'm a thousand per cent behind you, Sam,' I said. 'All these dirty stories going around about you, I know they ain't true, Sam, even if it sounds like they are, so you got my moral support a thousand per cent, and I'm goin' to be right up on the speaker's platform with you tonight to prove it!'

He said, 'Well, uh,' and cleared his throat awkwardly. He

said, 'Well, uh, that's certainly very nice of you, Sheriff. But, uh
– uh—'

What he wanted to say was that he didn't want me within a
thousand miles of him, let alone on the same speaker's platform.
But the kind of fella he was, he didn't know how to say it.

'Well – uh, now—' he tried again. 'I surely appreciate your
offer, Sheriff, but wouldn't it be better if, uh—'

I slapped him on the back, cutting him off. I said, by golly, I
was going to do it and he didn't need to worry about takin'
favors from me, because I wasn't really doin' him one.

'I figure it's just the right thing to do,' I said. 'You might say
it's something I got to do. So come tonight I'm goin' to be up
there on the platform with – *oof!*'

Zeke Carlton shoved past me, digging his elbow into my ribs.
He dropped an arm around Sam's shoulders, and jerked his
head at me.

'I'll say it for you, Sam. You don't want Nick around you,
because he's a sneaky, half-assed, triflin' no-good excuse for a
sheriff, and you'd be hurt just by bein' seen with him, even if
he didn't stick a knife in your ribs!'

Sam cleared his throat again, looking more uncomfortable
than ever. Zeke glared at me, like he wanted to spit in my face.

I said, 'Well, now Zeke, that ain't hardly no way to talk.
Here it is Sunday, and we're still here on the church grounds,
and god-dang if you ain't calling me names and using bad words
like "half-assed".'

'Balls!' he sneered. 'Who the hell are you to be correctin' me?
Why—'

'I'm the sheriff,' I said, 'an' it's my job to look out for wrong-
doin' particularly seein' that the Lord ain't abused right in His
own front yard. So you just better not do it no more, Zeke, or
I'll by-golly march you right down to the lock-up!'

Zeke let out an angry snort; laughed on a shaky note. He
looked around at the crowd, trying to swing them to his side.

But we're a real God-fearin' community, like you probably gathered, and everyone was frowning at him or givin' him frosty looks.

That made him madder than ever. 'Why, God da—, gosh-darn it, don't you see what he's trying to do? He's trying to get at Sam through me! He knows I'm backing Sam so he wants to make trouble for me!'

'Now, that just ain't so,' I said. 'You know it ain't so, Zeke.'

'The hell – the heck it ain't!'

I said, no, sir it sure wasn't and he knew it as well as I did. 'I leave it to anyone here,' I said, 'if they ever knew me to do a man dirty or even say so much as an unkind word about another fella as long as they've lived. Just ask anyone. I'll leave it up to them.'

Zeke scowled and muttered something under his breath. Cuss words, it sounded like. I asked Sam if he thought I was out to harm him, and he scuffled his feet and looked embarrassed.

'Well, uh, I'm sure you wouldn't, uh, do so – uh—'

'Right,' I said. 'I wouldn't. In the first place, it just ain't my nature to hurt another fella, an' in the second place I know it wouldn't do no good. Because I figure you can't be hurt, Sam. The way I see it, you're as good as elected right now.'

Sam's head snapped up. He kind of waved his hands, helplesslike, like he didn't know whether to pee or go blind. And if *he* was surprised, he sure had plenty of company. Everyone was staring at me, their eyes popped open. Even Zeke Carlton was struck dumb for a moment.

'Now, see here, Nick—' he spoke up at last. 'Now, let's get this straight. Are you saying that you're concedin' the election to Sam?'

'I'm saying that I'm going to,' I said, raising my voice. 'I'm concedin' to Sam just as soon as he answers one question.'

Zeke asked what kind of question. I said a very simple question, stalling a minute to get as big a crowd as I could.

'A very simple question,' I repeated. 'One that's already on everyone's lips, you might say, and that Sam would have to answer sooner or later.'

'Well, come on!' Zeke scowled impatiently. 'Ask it! Sam don't mind answering questions, do you, Sam? Sam's life is an open book!'

'How about that, Sam?' I said. 'I'd like to hear you speak for youself.'

Sam said, 'Well, uh, yes. I mean I'll be glad to answer your question. Uh, anything I can, that is.'

'Well, this is about them dirty stories people are tellin' on you,' I said. 'Now, wait a minute! Wait a minute, Zeke, Sam,' – I held up my hand – 'I know them stories ain't true. I know Sam wouldn't rape a little colored baby or steal the gold teeth out of his grandma's mouth or beat his pappy to death with a stick of cordwood or rob a widder woman of her life's savings or feed his wife to the hawgs. I *know* a fine fella like Sam wouldn't do nothing like that. So all I'm asking is this; this is my question . . .'

I paused again, gettin' everyone on their toes. I waited until you could have heard a weevil crapping on a cotton boll, and then I asked my question.

'All right,' I said, 'here it is. If them stories ain't true, how come them to get started? How come almost everybody claims they *are* true?'

Sam blinked. He opened his mouth, and then he closed it again. And he and Zeke looked at each other.

'Well, uh,' Sam began. 'I, uh, I—'

'Now, hold up there!' Zeke butted in, turning to me. 'What do you mean everybody's saying they're true? Who the hell's everybody?'

'I stand corrected,' I said. 'I reckon everybody ain't saying it, when you get right down to cases. Prob'ly ain't no more than two, three hundred people that are sayin' it. But that still leaves the same question. How come even two, three hundred people are sayin' it *is* true that Sam raped a little colored baby an' beat his pappy to death an' fed his wife to the hawgs an'—'

'Never mind, dammit!' Zeke grabbed Sam by the arm. 'Come on, Sam. You don't have to answer no damn-fool question like that.'

'Well, of course, he don't have to,' I said. 'But I should think he'd want to. Don't rightly see how he can get elected sheriff if he don't answer.'

Zeke hesitated, scowling. He shot a glance at Sam, then gave him a nudge.

'All right, Sam. Maybe you'd better answer.'

'Uh, well, of course,' Sam nodded. 'Uh, what was the question again, Sheriff?'

I started to tell him, but someone behind me interrupted.

'You know the question, Sam! How'd them stories about you get started? How come folks say they're true if they ain't?'

There was a loud murmur of agreement, with people nodding and nudging each other. Sam cleared his throat to speak, and there was another interruption. A catcall from the outskirts of the crowd.

'How about that nigger baby, Sam?'

The crowd looked at each other, embarrassed, snickering, or outright guffawing. All at once there were catcalls from half a dozen different directions.

'Where's them gold teeth, Sam?' and 'Did you just screw that widder for her money, Sam?' and 'What'd you do with them hawgs you fed your wife to?' and so on. Until everything was in an uproar of shouts and laughter and bootstampings.

I let it go on for two, three minutes, letting these here good Christians work themselves up to the proper pitch. Then I held up my arms and called for quiet, and finally I got it. But it was restless, you know. The kind of quiet you get just before a storm.

'Now, Sam,' I said, facing around to him again. 'You reckon you fully understand the question, or do you want me to repeat it?'

'Uh, well—'

'I'll repeat it,' I said, 'an' you listen closely, now, Sam. If you didn't rape any little defenseless colored babies or beat your poor ol' pappy to death or feed your sweet, trusting wife that you'd sworn to protect and cherish to the hawgs or – if you didn't do none of them dirty low-down things that make me sick to my stomach to think about, how come so many folks say you did? Or puttin' it briefly, Sam, how come folks say that you done things that would out-stink a skunk and that you're lower down than a puke-eating dawg, if it ain't true? Or puttin' it still another way, are you sayin' that you're telling the truth an' that everyone else is a dirty no-good liar?'

Zeke Carlton hollered, 'Now, wait a minute! That's not—' But he was hollered down before he could say anything more. Everyone was yelling for Sam to answer, to let him do his own talking. I held up my hands again.

'Well, Sam, what's the answer?' I said. 'We're all waitin' to hear it.'

'Well—' Sam wet his lips. 'Well, uh—'

'Yeah?' I said. 'Just speak right up, Sam. Why are people sayin' those stories are true, if they ain't?'

'Well . . .'

Sam didn't have an answer. You could almost smell him sweatin' blood to think of one, but he just couldn't. Which wasn't no surprise to me, of course, because how could anyone answer a question like that?

Sam kept trying, though. He was on maybe about his sixteenth try when someone flung a prayer book, hitting him spang in the mouth. And that was kind of like a signal, like the first crack of lightning in a storm. Because the air was suddenly full of prayer books and hymnals, and everyone was shouting and cussing and trying to get their hands on Sam. And all at once he disappeared like he'd been dropped through a trap door . . .

I sauntered on home.

I thought, well, it was just as well that I wouldn't be on the speaker's platform tonight at Sam's meeting because Sam wouldn't be there neither because there wouldn't be no meeting because Sam wouldn't be a candidate no more.

I thought, well, that was at least one nail out of my cross, and maybe, if I kept on being upright and Godfearin' and never hurting no one unless it was for their good or mine, which was pretty much the same thing, why then maybe all my other problems would get straightened out as easy as this one had.

We ate Sunday dinner, Rose and Myra and Lennie and me. Rose was supposed to go home that afternoon, and I said I'd sure be proud to take her as soon as I'd rested myself a little. But naturally I didn't take her.

I couldn't, you know, since I could only see her one more time. Just once to do something about her. And that plan had come back to me again – the plan for doing something about her and Lennie and Myra at the same time. But it wasn't something that I could pull off on Sunday afternoon, or any afternoon; it had to be at night. And, anyways, I had to study some more about it.

Myra called to me after about an hour. Then she came into my bedroom and called some more, shaking me until the whole bed almost fell apart. And, of course, it didn't do no good at all.

Finally, she gave up, and went back out into the other room, and I heard her apologizing to Rose.

'I simply can't wake him up, dear. He's just dead to the world. Not that it's any wonder, I suppose, considering how much sleep he's lost.'

Rose said, yes, it wasn't any wonder, was it?, her voice kind of flat. 'Well, I really hadn't planned on staying over tonight, but—'

'And you don't have to,' Myra declared. 'I'll just take Lennie and drive you home myself.'

'Now, that's not necessary,' Rose said quickly. 'I don't mind—'

'And I don't mind taking you. I really don't, darling. So you just get yourself ready – *Lennie, go wash your face* – and we'll be on our way.'

'Well,' said Rose. 'Well, all right, Myra, dear.'

They left a few minutes later.

I yawned and stretched and turned over on my side, all set to go to sleep for real. I started to doze, just started to, and I heard someone coming up the stairs.

It was a man, judging by the footsteps. I started to turn back on my side again, thinking, well, t'heck with him, it's Sunday afternoon an' I'm entitled to a little rest. But you just can't ignore no one when you're sheriff, Sunday or whatever day it is. So I flung my feet over the side of the bed, and got up.

I went out into the living room and flung open the hall door, just as he was about to knock on it.

He was a city-dressed fella, tall and thin with a nose like a fishhook and a mouth about as big as a bee's-ass.

'Sheriff Corey?' He flashed an identification card at me. 'I'm Barnes, the Talkington Detective Agency.'

He smiled, his bee's-ass mouth stretching enough to show one tooth, and it was like getting a glimpse of an egg coming out of a pullet pigeon. I said I was plumb proud to meet him.

'So you're with the Talkington Agency,' I said. 'Why, goddang if I ain't heard a lot about you people! Let's see now, you broke up that big railroad strike, didn't you?'

'That's right.' He showed me the tooth again. 'The railroad strike was one of our jobs.'

'Now, by golly, that really took nerve,' I said. 'Them railroad workers throwin' chunks of coal at you an' splashin' you with water, and you fellas without nothin' to defend yourself with except shotguns an' automatic rifles! Yes, sir, god-dang it, I really got to hand it to you!'

'Now, just a moment, Sheriff!' His mouth came together like a buttonhole. 'We have never—'

'And them low-down garment workers,' I said. 'God-dang, you really took care of them, didn't you? People that threw away them big three-dollar-a-week wages on wild livin' and then fussed because they had to eat garbage to stay alive! I mean, what the heck, they was all foreigners, wasn't they, and if they didn't like the good ol' American garbage, why didn't they go back where they came from?'

'Sheriff! Sheriff Corey!'

'Yeah?' I said. 'You got something on your mind, Mr Barnes?'

'Certainly I have something on my mind! Why else would I have come here? Now—'

'You mean you just didn't drop in for a little chat?' I said. 'Just to maybe show me your medals for shootin' people in the back an'—'

'I'm here to inquire about a former resident of Pottsville! A man named Cameron Tramell.'

'Never heard of him,' I said. 'Goodbye.'

I started to close the door, Barnes held it open.

'You've heard of him,' he said. 'He was known locally as Curly, and he was a pimp.'

I said, oh, I said, oh, yeah, sure, I'd heard of Curly. 'Ain't seen him for a spell, come to think of it. How's he getting along, anyways?'

'Now, Sheriff' – he grinned at me with his eyes – 'let's not spar with each other.'

'Spar? What do you mean?' I said.

'I mean, Cameron Trammel, alias Curly, is dead, as you well know. And you also know who killed him.'

20

had him come in, and we sat in the living room while he explained about Curly. It seemed that both bodies had been washed up, Moose's as well as Curly's. But no one was interested in Moose, whereas they were plenty interested in Curly. And the people that was interested in him was his own family, one of the best families in the South. They knew he was no good, naturally; in fact, they'd paid him to stay away from 'em. But still he was 'family' – still part of 'em – and they meant to see to it that his murderer was hanged.

'So here I am, Sheriff . . .' Barnes forced a smile. 'Perhaps we didn't see eye to eye on everything, but, well, I'm not a man to hold a grudge, and I'm sure neither of us wants to see a murderer running loose.'

'I know I sure don't,' I said. 'If I see any murderer runnin' around loose, I'll arrest 'em and throw 'em in jail.'

'Exactly. So if you'll tell me the name of the man who killed Curly . . .'

'Me?' I said. 'I don't know who killed him. If I did, I'd arrest him an' put—'

'Sheriff! You *do* know who killed him. You've admitted it.'

'Not me,' I said. '*You* said that I knew, not me.'

His mouth pinched together again, and his eyes along with it. With that fishhook nose, his face looked like three clods on a sandbank with a plough cutting through them.

'Approximately one week ago, on the morning after Curly was killed—'

'Now, how do you know it was the morning after?' I said. 'Ain't no one can say that unless it was the fella that killed him.'

'I know this, Sheriff. I know that your friend, Sheriff Ken Lacey, openly boasted on the streets of this town that he had taken care of Moose and Curly, meaning he had killed them. And you were with him at the time of this boasting, this claim that he had murdered those two men, and you gave your hearty approval to it.'

'Oh, yeah,' I laughed, 'now I remember. That was a little joke of Ken's an' mine. Had ourselves a peck of fun with it.'

'Now, Sheriff—'

'You think it wasn't?' I said. 'You think that a fella who'd killed two men would walk around the streets braggin' about it, and that I, an officer of the law, would just pat him on the back for it?'

'Never mind what I think, Sheriff! The events I have described *did* take place, and on the night previous to them – the only night Sheriff Lacey spent in Pottsville – he stayed at the river whorehouse, and he there boasted to the inmates of the house that he had fixed Moose and Curly good and that he had taken care of them good, and so on. In other words, there is incontrovertible evidence that approximately one week before Moose and Curly were found dead, on the *only* night Sheriff Lacey spent in Pottsville, he did declare himself to be the murderer of the aforesaid Moose and Curly.'

'Uh-hah,' I said, making myself sound real interested. 'Now, this in-con-tro-watchmacallit evidence you speak about. Would that be the unsupported word of these whorehouse gals?'

'It's not unsupported, dammit! There's Sheriff Lacey's bragging the following morning, and—'

'But he was just jokin', Mr Barnes. I put him up to it.'

Barnes' head snapped back, them little old eyes of his glaring at me. Then he darted it forward again, like he was going to hook me with his nose.

'Now, you listen to me, Corey! Listen to me good! I don't intend to – to—' He broke off suddenly, shook himself like a horse shaking off flies. Then his face twisted, and screwed up and unscrewed, and god-dang if he didn't smile. 'Please excuse me, Sheriff Corey; I've had a rather trying day. I'm afraid I lost track of the fact, for a moment, that we're both equally sincere and intent in our desire for justice even though we may not act and think alike.'

I nodded and said that I guessed he was right all right. He beamed and went on.

'Now, you've known Sheriff Lacey for years. He's a good friend of yours. You naturally feel that you have to protect him.'

'Uh-uh,' I said. 'He ain't a friend of mine, and if there was any way I could pin them two murders on him I'd be plain proud to do it.'

'But, Sheriff—'

'He *was* a friend of mine,' I said. 'He stopped bein' one even before that night he came down here an' rousted me out of bed and got me to point out the way to the whorehouse to him.'

'Then he did go there!' Barnes rubbed his hands together. 'You can testify of your own knowledge that he did go to the whorehouse on the night in question?'

'Why, sure I can,' I said. 'It's the plain truth, so why couldn't I testify to it?'

'But that's wonderful! Wonderful, Sheriff! And did Lacey tell you why he wanted to go to the – no, wait a minute. Did he say anything that would indicate that he was going to the whorehouse for the purpose of killing Moose and Curly?'

'You mean then, that night?' I shook my head. 'No, he didn't say anything then.'

'But he did at some other time! When?'

'That day,' I said, 'when I was over to his county on a visit.

He said that pimps was one thing he just didn't have no use for, and that he believed in killin' 'em on general principles.'

Barnes jumped up, and began pacing around the room. He said that what I'd told him was wonderful, wonderful, and it was just what he needed, then, stopped in front of me an' shook his finger sort of playful.

'You're quite a tease, Sheriff. Almost made me lose my temper, and I'm a man who prides himself on self-control. You had this vital information all along, and yet you appeared to be defending Lacey.'

I said that, well, that was the way I was, a real card. He glanced at his watch, and asked me what time he could get a train into the city.

'Oh, you got lots of time,' I said. 'Better'n a couple of hours. Best thing you can do is stay an' have supper with us.'

'Why – Why, that's very kind of you, Sheriff. Very kind.'

I got some whiskey out of the office, and we had ourselves a few drinks. He started talking about himself, him and the detective agency, me throwing in a word now and then by way of leading him on, and his voice began to get kind of bitter. It seemed like he hated what he was doing. He knew exactly what Talkington was, and he couldn't make no excuses for it. It was a downright hateful outfit, and he was part of its hateful doings, and he hated himself because he was.

'You probably know what I mean, Sheriff. Even a man in your job has to close his eyes to some very bad things.'

'You're right about that,' I said. 'I have to close 'em if I want to stay on bein' sheriff.'

'And do you want to? You've never thought of taking up another line of work?'

'Not for very long,' I said. 'What else would a fella like me do anyways?'

'Exactly!' His eyes lit up and they began to look a lot bigger. 'What else can you do? What else can I do? But, Nick – excuse me for being familiar – my name's George, Sheriff.'

'Glad to know you, George,' I nodded, 'an' you go right on calling me Nick.'

'Thank you, Nick' – he took another drink of whiskey. 'Now, here's what I was going to ask, Nick and it's something I've worried about a great deal. Does the fact that we can't do anything else – does that excuse us?'

'Well,' I said, 'do you excuse a post for fittin' a hole? Maybe there's a nest of rabbits down in that hole, and the post will crush 'em. But is that the post's fault, for fillin' a gap it was made to fit?'

'But that's not a fair analogy, Nick. You're talking about inanimate objects.'

'Yeah?' I said. 'So ain't we all relatively inanimate, George? Just how much free will does any of us exercise? We got controls all along the line, our physical make-up, our mental make-up, our backgrounds; they're all shapin' us a certain way, fixin' us up for a certain role in life, and George, we better play that role or fill that hole or any god-dang way you want to put it or all hell is going to tumble out of the heavens and fall right down on top of us. We better do what we were made to do, or we'll find it being done to us.'

'You mean it's a case of kill or be killed?' Barnes shook his head. 'I hate to think that, Nick.'

'Maybe that's not what I mean,' I said. 'Maybe I'm not sure what I mean. I guess mostly what I mean is that there can't be no personal hell because there ain't no personal sins. They're all public, George, we all share in the other fellas' and the other fellas all share in ours. Or maybe I mean this, George, that I'm the savior himself, Christ on the Cross come right here to Potts County, because God knows I was needed here, an' I'm goin' around doing kindly deeds – so that people will know they got nothing to fear, and if they're worried about hell they don't have to dig for it. And, by God, that makes sense, don't it, George? I mean obligation ain't all on the side of the fella that accepts it, nor responsibility neither. I mean, well, which is worse, George, the fella that craps on a doorknob or the one that rings the doorbell?'

George threw back his head and roared with laughter. 'That's priceless, Nick! Priceless!'

'Well, it ain't exactly original,' I said. 'Like the poem says, you can't fault a jug for bein' twisted because the hand of the potter slipped. So you tell me which is worse, the one that messes up the doorknob or the one that rings the bell, and I'll tell you which got twisted and who done the twisting.'

'But – but suppose the same person does both?'

'It ain't likely,' I said. 'As a fella that's had to deal with plenty of high jinks, and god-dang if I don't feel I'm living in a joker's paradise sometimes. I can say that these little chores is usually divided up. But if that wasn't the case, George, then we've opened up another field of obligation and responsibility. Because this fella had to eat before he could crap, didn't he. and where did the food come from?'

We went on talking and drinking until Myra came home.

She fixed dinner for George and me, she an' Lennie having already eaten at Rose's place. George was real courtly to Myra. God-dang if she didn't look almost pretty the way he shined up to her, and god-dang if he didn't look almost handsome because he done it.

Then we finished eating and I walked George toward the railroad station, and things weren't so nice any more. We were friendly, but it was just one of those have-to-be things. There wasn't no real warmth or liking in it.

I reckon that's the bad part of whiskey, you know? – the bad part about a lot of things. Not the indulging of 'em, but the not being able to indulge. The afterwards, when the ol' familiar taste of piss is back in your mouth, and you want to spit it out at everyone. And you think, god-dang, why for did I want to be nice to that fella? And I bet he thought I was a god-danged fool.

George was looking kind of glum and let-down; kind of frowny and thoughtful. Then, Amy Mason crossed to our side of the street, and I introduced her, and George perked himself up again.

'You have a fine sheriff, here,' he said, clapping me on the back. 'A very fine officer, Miss Mason. He's helped me solve a very important case.'

'Indeed?' said Amy. 'What kind of case, Mr Barnes?'

And George told her, adding on that he just wouldn't have had a case against Ken if it hadn't been for me.

'I'm sure it wasn't an easy thing for him to do, either,' he said. 'It's never easy for one officer to incriminate another, even if they are not friends.'

'How true!' Amy said. 'And I'm sure it will become even less easy as time goes on. By the way, Sheriff, will you stop by my house this evening? I think I've seen a prowler around.'

I said I'd be tickled to death to stop by, and she mustn't feel like she had to set out no coffee or cake or nothing because I wouldn't want her troubled.

She said she wouldn't be troubled at all, sort of tossing her head at me. Then, she went on, and George Barnes and I went on toward the station.

Way up river, the train was whistling for the crossing. George shook my hand and gave me a bee's-ass smile, and thanked me again for my help.

'By the way, Nick. It's just a matter of form, of course, but you'll be receiving a subpoena within the next day or so.'

'A subpoena?' I said. 'Why for will I be receiving one of those?'

'As a prosecution witness against Ken Lacey, naturally! The chief prosecution witness, I should say. We'd certainly never get a conviction without you.'

'But what am I going to testify against him about?' I said. 'What's old Ken supposed to have went and done?'

'*What's he supposed to have done?*' George stared at me. 'Why – what are you trying to pull, anyway? You know what he's done!'

'Well, now I reckon I forgot,' I said. 'Maybe you wouldn't mind tellin' me again?'

'Now you see here!' He grabbed me by the shoulders, teeth gritted. 'Don't you go dumb on me, Corey. If you want money, all right, but—'

'I'm really plumb puzzled, George.' I eased out of his grip. 'Why for would I want money?'

'For stating under oath what you've already told me privately. That Ken Lacey murdered Cameron Tramell, alias Curly!'

'Huh?' I said. 'Now, wait a minute, George. I didn't tell you nothin' like that.'

'Oh, yes, you did! You certainly did tell me that, in so many words. You told me—'

'Well, maybe you got that impression,' I said. 'But never mind about that, never mind what I told you. The important thing, I reckon, is what I didn't tell you.'

'And what was that?'

'This,' I said. 'The morning after Ken Lacey left, I saw Moose an' Curly alive.'

21

It was Sunday morning. Early-early Sunday morning. Way off somewhere in the country, I could hear a rooster crowing, but I figured he was probably just dumb – or doing it for exercise, because it was at least an hour before dawn.

Yes, sir, it was plumb quiet, and not a creature was stirring, you might say. Except for me, shifting my buttocks a little on the bed now and then so's I would stay comfortable. And except for Rose.

She was out in the kitchen, it sounded like, fixing herself a cup of coffee. Then there was a clattery-clash, and I reckoned she must have thrown the cup against the wall, and then I heard a mumbled string of words that had to be curses.

I yawned and stretched. I sure was needing some sleep, but I guess I'm always in need of sleep like I'm always in need of food. Because my labors were mighty ones – ol' Hercules didn't know what hard work was – and what is there to do but eat and sleep? And when you're eatin' and sleepin' you don't have to fret about things that you can't do nothing about. And what else is there to do but laugh an' joke . . . how else can you bear up under the unbearable?

It was a cinch that cryin' didn't do no good. I'd tried that before in my agony – I'd cried out as loud as a fella could cry – an' it hadn't done no good at all.

I yawned and stretched again.

Sunday in Pottsville, I thought. Sunday in Pottsville, an' my sweetheart is going to leave me, and I hope it don't grieve me. My eyes plumb deceive me, an' no one'll believe me.

And I thought, god-dang it, Nick, if you didn't already have your work cut out for you, you could be a poet. The poet laureate of Potts County, by dang, and you could make up poems about piss tinkling in pots and jaybirds with the bots and assholes tying knots and . . .

Rose came in, and stood beside my bed.

She looked down at me, biting her lip, her face twisted like a handful of clay that a baby has played with.

'I just want to tell you one thing, Nick Corey,' she said. 'And don't think you're not getting off lucky, because I'd be doing a lot more than talk to you if I could. I'd see you swinging by your neck, you dirty bastard. I'd tell about you killing Tom, and goddam you, I'd laugh my head off when they strung you up, an' – an'—'

'I thought you were just going to tell me one thing,' I said. 'Seems to me like that's about a dozen.'

'Screw you! I'm not going to tell you what I was going to say because I'm a decent woman. But if I wasn't, you know what I'd say? You know what I'd do to you, you rotten son-of-a-bitch? I'd heist a leg and pee in your ear until it washed out that stinking pile of crap you call brains!'

'Now, you just watch out now, Rose,' I said. 'You just better watch out or you'll be saying something dirty.'

She started bawling, and stumbled back out of the room.

I heard her as she dropped down on the lounge, bawling and sniffling. And after a while she began to mumble to herself. Wondering out loud how *anyone* – meaning me – could do such a terrible thing.

And what could I have said except that it wasn't easy; it sure wasn't easy. And how could I explain what I didn't really understand myself?

Well?

But this is what had happened.

22

After I'd taken George Barnes to the station last Sunday, I stopped by Amy Mason's house. I knew I'd better explain that I'd just been kidding in front of Barnes – that I didn't have no intention of letting Ken Lacey get blamed for killing those pimps. But the way she hopped on me the minute I showed up, I hardly had a chance to say anything.

'I warned you, Nick!' she blazed at me. 'I warned you not to do it! Now, you'll have to bear the consequences!'

'Now, wait a minute, honey,' I said. 'What—'

'I'm going to send a telegram to the governor, that's what! Right tonight! I'm going to tell him who actually did kill those two, uh, men!'

'But Amy, I didn't—'

'I'm sorry, Nick. You'll never know how sorry I am. But I'm going to do it. I can't allow you to commit a murder – and framing Sheriff Lacey would be murder – that I know about in advance.'

I finally managed to make her listen to me, to tell her that I wasn't even halfway planning to frame Ken. 'It was just a joke, see? I was just leadin' Barnes on for a good hard letdown.'

'Yes?' She looked at me sharply. 'You're sure about that?'

'Sure I'm sure. You should have seen his face when I told him I'd seen them pimps alive the day after Ken was down there.'

'Well . . .'

She was still sort of suspicious, still not quite convinced that I didn't have some scheme for framing Ken without getting myself in trouble. Finally, I got kind of impatient, and I said I wasn't really flattered to have her doubtin' my word when she didn't have no reason to.

'I'm sorry.' She smiled and pecked me on the cheek. 'I believe you, dear, and I'll tell you something else. If I hated Sheriff Lacey like you do, I'd probably want to kill him, too!'

'Hate?' I said. 'What makes you think I hate him?'

'Now, darling, it sticks out all over you. What did he ever do to you to make you feel that way about him?'

'But I don't,' I said. 'I mean, I don't hate him. I mean, it ain't what I feel about him that matters. It's what he is, you know; the things he's done to others. I – well, it's kind of hard to explain but – but—'

'Never mind, dear.' She laughed and kissed me again. 'You're not going to do anything to him, and that's all that matters.'

But it wasn't all, you know? Not by a long shot. I'd've sworn that I never held no malice toward no one, never a speck of hatred. Or if I ever had felt sort of a teensy twinge of dislike, it hadn't been the motivatin' factor in whatever I'd done.

That's the way I felt about myself, anyways, until Amy'd said what she'd said. And now I was kind of worried. I could put Ken Lacey out of my mind, since I wasn't going to take any action against him. But the others, well, they were all part of the same pattern, weren't they? And if I'd been showing spite toward Ken, then maybe I'd been doing the same thing with them.

And maybe, in the case of what I was about to do, the people I was about to take care of . . .

But it had to be done, I reckoned. It had to be, and I didn't have no choice in the matter.

I was willing to let things ride; I'm long sufferin', you might say. But they wouldn't have it that way.

Rose was callin' Myra every day, hinting that she needed me

to do this or that for her. And Myra kept naggin' at me to go out and do what Rose wanted done (which wasn't what Myra thought it was). And Amy was insistin' that I couldn't see Rose but one more time – no more, or else. And Lennie had taken one of his spells of tagging after me, and spying on me. And—

And finally it was Saturday night, last night, and I couldn't hold out no longer. They were all asking for it! And like the Good Book says, Ask and ye shall receive.

It was about eight in the evening, about an hour after sunset.

I came running down the cotton rows, half-stooped, which didn't conceal me much because it was a low stand of cotton. In the dusk, just about anyone nearby could see me, and they didn't even have to be too nearby. And that was the way I wanted it.

Lennie didn't like to walk. Ordinarily, he'd never go outside the town limits. It had really been a job to act sneaky and creepy enough to tote him way out here to Rose's place.

I came out of the cotton, and made a dash toward the house. Out of the corner of my eye, I could see Lennie rising up in the field. Gawking openly, as I reached the house and pounded on the door. He really thought he had me now, Lennie did; he had me and Rose. He'd caught me sneaking into her house at night, so pretty soon now he was going to do some peeking. And then he'd go back to town with a fine story to tell Myra. A real juicy story about her own husband and her best friend.

That was just the way I wanted it.

That was the way I'd planned it.

Lennie was going to get a story for Myra, all right, but it would be a lot nastier than he figured on.

'Nick—' Rose opened the door. 'What – where have you been, anyway? Why didn't you come out last—'

'Later.' I squeezed inside and closed the door. I kissed her, keeping her mouth closed until I knew she was ready to listen. 'I couldn't come any sooner, honey, because I been workin' on a plan. It's a way to get rid of Myra and Lennie, and I've already taken the first step an' now I'm goin' to need your help. So here I am, askin' for it. You don't want to give it, you just say so and we'll just forget all about gettin' rid of 'em and go on like we been doin'.'

'But, by – what—' She was willing but confused, puzzled. I'd talked fast, acting excited and running my words together, and I had her nodding even while she was frowning and wondering what the heck it was all about.

'Well, forget it,' I said, turning toward the door. 'Just forget I asked, Rose, an' I'm sorry I troubled you.'

'No, wait! Wait, honey!' She grabbed onto me. 'I just wondered what – why – but I'll do it, honey! You just tell me what it is!'

'I want you to wait a couple of minutes,' I said. 'Then, I want you to go outside and grab Lennie an'—'

'Lennie!' She let out a frightened gasp. 'D-Did he—'

'He followed me out here. I egged him into doin' it, because that's part of the plan. So you grab him and haul him inside, and then you tell him what I tell you to.'

I told her what to say, the gist of it, that is. She turned pale, lookin' at me like I'd gone out of my mind.

'N-Nick! That's – that's crazy! I couldn't—'

'Sure, it's crazy,' I said. 'It's got to be crazy, don't you see?'

'But . . . oh,' she said, and her eyes narrowed a little. 'Yeah, I can see how it might – but, Nick, honey, what about the rest? How does—'

'There ain't time to tell you, now,' I said. 'You just go on an' take care of Lennie, an' I'll explain everything afterwards.'

I turned and went into the bedroom, seeming to take it for granted, you know, that she'd do what I told her to.

She stayed where she was for a moment, fidgeting uncertainly. Frowning and maybe a little frightened. She took a step toward the bedroom, on the point, it looked like, of calling out to me. Then she suddenly faced back around, crossed to the door, and went outside.

Dimly, I heard running sounds. The fast scuffle of footsteps on the hard-packed clay of the yard. I heard a holler as she grabbed hold of Lennie, and I heard him burbling and giggling as she dragged him into the house. Tickled pink with himself, but just a mite scared along with it.

They came into the kitchen. I stood back out of sight, watching and listening.

'All right,' Rose said, her eyes pure poison as she looked at him. 'What were you doing sneaking around here?'

Lennie giggled and smirked, putting his hands over his mouth, lattice-like. Then, he said me an' Rose was really going to catch it.

'You just wait, I'm gonna tell Myra on you! I seen him! I seen ol' smarty Nick! He come sneaking out here so's you 'n' him could do somethin' nasty!'

'You mean screwing?' Rose said. 'What's nasty about screwing?'

'Ooh!' Lennie pointed a shaky finger at her, his eyes popped as big as saucers. 'Now, you done it! You're really gonna catch it now! I tell Myra you—'

'What's the matter?' Rose said. 'You screw Myra all the time, and don't tell me you don't, you stupid-looking jackass! That's what makes you goofy, banging her so much. You've tossed it to her so often you've thrown your ass out of line with your eyeballs!'

I almost busted out laughing.

That Rose! There just wasn't no one like her, god-dang it! In less than a minute, now, she'd got Lennie so mixed up that he couldn't have found his butt if it'd had a bell on it.

He pointed his finger at her again, shaking all over. Rubbing his eyes with his other hand as he started to blubber.

'I *deed* not! I do not! I never done nothin' like that, an'—'

'The hell you didn't! You're not her brother, you're her boy friend! That's what she keeps you around for, to diddle her fiddle. Because you're low-hung and she's high-strung!'

'It a-ain't n-neither! I *de-ed* not! You – y-you're just a m-mean ol' storyteller, an'—'

'Don't lie to me, you liver-lipped bastard!' Rose shook her fist in his face. 'I've seen you pouring it on her! I climbed up one of those ladders the painters are using and peeked in the window, and goddam, you were pounding it like a drum. The way you were banging the bunghole, you damned near fell in!'

Well, god-dang. It was better than a circus. And it just went to show what a fella could do when he really put his mind to it.

Here you take a common everyday thing like fornication, which, like the fella says, can be a pretty fleeting pleasure. But if you can just take the idea of it, you know, and start tossing it around amongst the right people, or the wrong ones, dependin' on your viewpoint, why then you can get something pretty god-dang unusual. Something like what was going on here.

A heck of a lot of laughs – plus the means of getting some people to get rid of themselves, when there ain't no way for you to get rid of them.

'I'm g-gonna tell M-Myra!' Lennie blubbered. 'I'll tell jus' what you said about her, every dirty m-mean word an'—'

'Cow's ass?' said Rose, like she was sayin' 'How's that?' and, 'Suck which?' Like she was sayin' 'Says which?' 'You and Myra better stop playing tickle the pickle, boy, before you bat your brains out with your balls.'

'I'm gonna tell Myra!' Lennie bawled, stumbling toward the door. 'You're gonna get it!'

'Tell her she may be a hole, but you're no post,' Rose said. 'Tell her you'll tickle her ass if she'll whistle "Old Black Joe".'

She gave Lennie a shove. It knocked him clean out the door and off the porch, and he landed sprawling in the yard.

He picked himself up, blubbering and rubbing his eyes. Rose gave him a final cussing, accusing him and Myra of a whole blast of dirty things. It kind of made me wince to listen to her, it was that dirty. What she'd said before sounded downright complimentary by comparison.

She came back in, slamming the door. I gave her a hug, and told her she'd done just fine.

'Now, are you beginnin' to get the picture?' I said. 'Lennie never leaves town. He's not only too danged lazy to do any real walkin', but he's scared to get very far off by himself. Myra knows this. She knows he'd be just about as likely to flap his arms and fly as he would to come way out here to your place. So what happens when he goes home and tells Myra he *has* been out here?'

Rose said, 'Mmm,' nodding her head slowly. 'She probably won't believe him, right? But what—'

'She won't believe him,' I said. 'Leastways, she'll have some awful strong doubts he's telling the truth. Then, he tells her all the dirty things you said about her, about her and Lennie sleepin' together and so on. And how can she believe that? How can she believe that her very best friend, a perfect lady, would all of a sudden start talking dirty about her?'

'Mmm-hmm,' Rose nodded again. 'She can't believe that he came out here, in the first place, and she can't believe what he says happened here. The way she sees it, he'll just have made it all up, and he'll probably get his ears boxed for lying. But—'

'Not just lying,' I said, 'but god-danged dangerous lyin'. The kind that breaks up homes, and gets people killed. And Myra won't want to chance the risk of it happening again. She'll figure he's taken a real bad turn for the worse, and she'll have to put him away somewhere like she's sometimes threatened to.'

'Huh!' Rose gave me a startled look. 'When did Myra ever do anything like that? Why she can hardly bear to let Lennie out of her sight!'

I said Myra had threatened to put him away a couple times, when she got extra mad at him, and, yeah, she couldn't hardly bear to let Lennie out of sight. 'That's why she's never done anything about him, because she'd want to be with him wherever he was and she didn't want to leave Pottsville. Now, though, she's got no choice. He goes and she goes, too.'

Rose said she just wasn't sure about it. It sounded good but you couldn't depend on it working out that way. I said that, well, of course we'd have to help things along a little.

'Myra's bound to tell us about it, and naturally, we get pretty blamed worried. And the worrieder we get the worrieder she gets. We're real concerned about what Lennie might do next, you know, like maybe taking a meat axe to people instead of just lying about 'em. Or setting houses on fire. Or chasin' little girls. Or – well, don't you fret about it, honey.' I gave her a squeeze, and a pat on the bottom. 'Everything's goin' to work out fine, but absolutely fine. I ain't got a doubt in the world about it.'

Rose shrugged and said, well, maybe so, I knew Myra better than she did. Then, she snuggled up to me and bit my ear. And I kissed her, and pulled myself away.

'Lennie ain't a real fast walker,' I explained. 'I aim to cut cross-country and beat him back to town. Just in case, you know.'

'Just in case?' Rose frowned. 'In case of what?'

'In case we need a clincher. Something that'll sweep the last doubt out of Myra's mind, if she should have a doubt. It ain't even remotely likely that she will have. But when Lennie gets to the courthouse, just pantin' to tell Myra about me bein' out here, ain't it a pretty good idea for me to be sittin' in my office?'

Rose had to admit that it was, much as she hated to have me leave.

I promised we'd get together in a day or so. Then, I beat it out the door before I had to talk any more.

Naturally, I didn't go back to town. I already knew what was going to happen there. What I wanted to see was what was going to happen here, although I already had a pretty good idea, and maybe to help it along a little if it needed helpin'.

I circled around through the fields until I reached the lane that came up from the road. Then, I hunkered down beside it in a clump of scrub mulberries, and waited.

About an hour and a half passed. I started to worry a little, wonderin' if I could have been wrong, and then I heard the squeak of buggy wheels coming on fast.

I parted the bushes and peeked out. Lennie and Myra swept by, Myra clutching the horse's reins, Lennie's head lolling back and forth on his neck. He was carrying something on his lap, a black, box-like thing, and one of his hands clutched something that looked like a stick. I scratched my head, wonderin' what the heck the stuff was – the box and the stick – and then the buggy had rolled past me, up and out of the lane and into the farmyard.

Myra whoa-ed the horse to a stop. She and Lennie climbed down from the buggy, and she trailed the reins over the horse's head to keep it from wandering away. Then, she and Lennie crossed the yard and went up on the porch.

She banged on the door. It opened after a minute, and the lamplight outlined her face, white and purposeful-looking. She started to go in, then she took Lennie by the shoulder and shoved him in ahead of her. And at last I saw what he was carryin'.

It was a camera – a camera and one of them sticks that you explode flash-powder in for taking pictures indoors.

23

I jumped up and started for the house. About the first step I took, my foot caught in a root and I fell sprawling with the wind knocked out of me. For a minute or two, I didn't even have enough breath to groan, and when I finally did manage to pick myself up, I couldn't move very fast. So it was maybe all of five minutes before I got to the house, and found a window where I could hear and see.

Well, sir, it was a funny thing, a funny-terrible thing, a strange crazy thing. Because what caught my attention wasn't what you'd have thought it would be at all. Not Rose, scared and dazed and wonderin' what the heck had gone wrong. Not Lennie and Myra, smilin' and spiteful and enjoyin' theirselves. Not something that was in the room itself. Not somethin' but nothing. The emptiness. The absence of things.

I'd maybe been in that house a hundred times, that one and a hundred others like it. But this was the first time I'd seen what they really were. Not homes, not places for people to live in, not nothin'. Just pine-board walls locking in the emptiness. No pictures, no books – nothing to look at or think about. Just the emptiness that was soakin' in on me here.

And then suddenly it wasn't here, it was everywhere, every place like this one. And suddenly the emptiness was filled with sound and sight, with all the sad terrible things that the emptiness had brought the people to.

There were the helpless little girls, cryin' when their own daddies crawled into bed with 'em. There were the men beating their wives, the women screamin' for mercy. There were the kids wettin' in the beds from fear and nervousness, and their mothers dosin' 'em with red pepper for punishment. There were the haggard faces, drained white from hookworm and blotched with scurvy. There was the near-starvation, the never-bein'-full, the debts that always outrun the credits. There was the how-we-gonna-eat, how-we-gonna-sleep, how-we-gonna-cover-our-poor-bare-asses thinkin'. The kind of thinkin' that when you ain't doing nothing else but that, why you're better off dead. Because that's the emptiness thinkin' and you're already dead inside, and all you'll do is spread the stink and the terror, the weepin' and wailin', the torture, the starvation, the shame of your deadness. Your emptiness.

I shuddered, thinking how wonderful was our Creator to create such downright hideous things in the world, so that something like murder didn't seem at all bad by comparison. Yea, verily, it was indeed merciful and wonderful of Him. And it was up to me to stop brooding, and to pay attention to what was going on right here and now.

So I made an extra hard try, rubbing my eyes and shaking myself, and finally I managed to.

'—a goddam liar!' Rose was yelling. 'I didn't say any such of a goddam thing!'

'Tsk, tsk.' There was a possum grin on Myra's face. 'Such language. I'm beginning to think you're not a very nice girl, after all.'

'To hell with what you think! Who wouldn't cuss, having you and that idiot show up at this time of night!'

'You mean you didn't expect us?' Myra said. 'Did you think I'd let you talk that way about me, and not do anything about it?'

'But I didn't talk about you! Lennie's lyin! Lennie wasn't even out here tonight!'

'Wasn't he? Then what was his handkerchief doing out there

on the porch? One of the extra-big, double-thick kind I make for him because the poor dear's always slobbering.'

Myra went on grinning, watching the fear spread over Rose's face. Rose stammered that she was lying, that she hadn't found Lennie's handkerchief on the porch. But she had, all right. I'd put it there myself.

'Well?' Myra said. 'Well, Rose?'

Rose was caught, and she must have known it. The rough talk she'd been using was a dead giveaway in itself. But like a scared person will, she kept on trying.

'W-Well . . .' She bobbed her head jerkily. 'All right, Lennie *was* here. I caught him sneaking around the house and it scared me, and I guess I talked pretty rough to him. But – but I certainly didn't say those dirty things that he says I did!'

'Didn't you?'

'No, I didn't! How many times do I have to tell you?'

Myra laughed, a mean scary laugh that even made me shiver. She said that Rose didn't have to tell her any times, because a lie didn't gain anything by repetition.

'Lennie's telling the truth, dear. He doesn't have the imagination to make up a story like that.'

'B-But – but—'

'And you don't have the imagination either. You couldn't have invented the story, any more than he could. Which means – well, I don't know how you found out, but you obviously did. And that's the important thing, isn't it? That and making sure that you don't do any talking to anyone else.'

Rose stared at her, slowly shaking her head, her voice a harsh sickish whisper. 'I – I d-don't believe you. Y-You and Lennie. *I just don't believe you!*'

The fact was, I was pretty shocked myself. Because I'd guessed the truth; I'd been pretty sure of it. But that wasn't nowhere near the same as knowin' it.

'I don't believe you,' Rose repeated shakily. 'Why – why would you—'

'Oh, stop pretending,' Myra said. 'You found out about us, and you were foolish enough to tell Lennie. As for the why of things, you're going to find that out, too, and very shortly. That is, of course, if you're similarly attracted to him.'

She motioned to Lennie. He fastened the camera around her neck with a strap, and she fiddled with the settings for a minute, getting it like she wanted. Then he poured powder into the flashstick from a can in his pocket, and carefully handed it to her.

Rose stood staring at them.

Myra let out another one of her mean-scary laughs. 'Don't worry about your picture, dear. I'm really quite professional with a camera. In fact, I made quite a bit of money that way before I was married, quite a bit. You'd be surprised at the sums people paid me for certain pictures that I took of them.'

Rose shook her head, seeming to shake off her fear for the moment. She said that Myra was going to get a surprise if she didn't drag her ass out of there.

'Now, beat it, you baggy old bitch! Take your buggy boy friend and clear out of here before I forget I'm a lady!'

'In a moment, dear. Just as soon as I take your picture – with Lennie.'

'Take my picture! Why, goddam you—'

'Mmm-hmm, take your picture. With Lennie. It'll be much safer than killing you, and every bit as effective at keeping you quiet, and – *tear her clothes off, Lennie!*'

Lennie's hand darted out before Rose could move. It caught in the front of her dress and ripped downward, taking the underclothes along with the dress. Before you could blink an eye, she was standing in a puddle of rags, naked as a baby jay.

Lennie burbled and choked on his own spit, and about a pint more spilled over his chin. Myra gave him a lovin' look.

'She looks very good, doesn't she, darling? Why don't you see if she really is?'

'Guh, guh—' Lennie hesitated doubtfully. 'M-Maybe she hurt me?'

'Now, of course she won't hurt you,' Myra laughed. 'You're big and she's little, and anyway I'm here to protect you.'

'Guh, guh—' Lennie still hesitated. He'd ripped Rose's clothes off, but just doing that, just the one quick grab, didn't take much guts. He wasn't quite ready to go the rest of the way, even with Myra to nerve him up and tell him it was okay. 'W-What – how I do it, Myra?'

'Just grab her and throw her down,' Myra said, and then, sharply, forcing him to obey before he could think, '*Grab her, Lennie!*'

Rose had been standin' sort of stunned since her clothes were ripped off. Glazed-eyed, too stupefied even to try to cover herself.

But then Lennie grabbed, hugging her to him, slobbering over her, and everything was changed. She came to life like a turpentined bobcat, screaming, clawing, kicking and pounding. Lennie got hit and clawed in about a dozen places at the same time, not to mention a kneein' in his crotch and a kicking on his shins.

He fell away from her, blubbering and clutching himself. Rose darted into the bedroom and slammed the door, and Myra hauled off and kicked Lennie in the tail.

'You big boob, go after her! Break the door down!'

'I'm a-scairt,' Lennie whined. 'She hurt me!'

'I'll hurt you a lot worse!' Myra twisted his ear by way of demonstration. 'I'll beat you black and blue if you don't do what I tell you. *Now, break that door down!*'

Lennie began to shoulder the door. Myra stood right behind him, urging him on, telling him what would happen if he didn't mind her.

The lock gave. The door banged open, Lennie following it with his rush and Myra following him. And . . .

And so I reckon I never will know what was in Myra's mind.

Or what wasn't in it. Whether she'd forgot about that pistol she'd helped Rose buy, or whether she thought that Rose wouldn't dare use it. Or whether she was so danged mad and determined to put Rose in a fix that she just wasn't thinking.

No, sir, I'll never know what she thought or didn't think. Because just about a second after the bedroom door busted open, she and Lennie were dead.

They came stumbling backward into the living room when Rose started shooting, falling over each other, going down to the floor together in a tangled heap. They were already dead then, I reckon, but Rose kept on firing – like she was shooting fish in a barrel – until the gun was empty.

I climbed in the buggy and started for town, ponderin' over the strange workings of Providence. What I'd really sort of figured on was that Myra would kill Rose, and then Myra and Lennie would have to skip town, because I would be absolutely impartial even if they were sort of kinfolks and I'd do my dangdest to see that they were punished even if I had to shoot 'em while they were trying to escape. Which would probably be the best way of winding things up.

But this would be all right, I reckoned. It would work out just as well with Rose killin' Myra and Lennie.

I put the horse and buggy in the livery stable, listening to the hostler snore away in the hayloft. I went back across town to the courthouse, and everyone was long-gone in bed of course and it was like there wasn't no one on the earth but me.

I went upstairs to the living quarters, and drew the shades down tight. Then, I lit a lamp and got myself a cup of cold coffee from the stove, and eased down on the lounge to drink it.

I finished it, and carried the cup back into the kitchen. I toed my boots off and stretched out on the lounge to rest. And the downstairs door slammed open and Rose came pounding up the steps and busted in on me.

She'd run all the way into town on foot, I reckon, and she

was wild-eyed and crazy-lookin'. She sagged against the door, heaving for breath, pointing a shaking accusin' finger at me. It was all she could do for a moment, just point.

I said howdy-do to her, and then I said it was all right, me and her bein' friends, but it really wasn't perlite to point at people.

'I thought you ought to know that,' I said. 'It not only ain't polite. but you might poke someone in the eye.'

'Y-You!' she said, fighting for breath. 'You – you—!'

'Or if they was real tall folks,' I said, 'you might poke 'em in some other bodily orifice, which could be plumb embarrassin' for you, not to mention the danger of getting your finger caught.'

She took a long, shuddery heave. Then she came over to the lounge and stood over me. 'You you you son-of-a-bitch" she said. 'You you you rotten stinking bastard. You – you goddamned whoremongering, double-crossing, low-down, worthless, no-good, mean, hateful, two-timing onery—'

'Now, god-dang it, Rose,' I said. 'Danged if it don't almost sound as if you was mad at me.'

'*Mad!*' she yelled. 'I'll show you how mad I am! I'll—'

'Better not holler so loud!' I said. 'Folks might be roused into coming up here to find out what's going on.'

Rose said to let 'em come, but she lowered her voice. 'I'll damned well tell them what's going on, you dirty bastard! I'll tell them just what happened!'

'And what would that be?' I said.

'Don't you play dumb on me, damn you! You *know* what happened! You were outside all the time, because I heard you when you drove away! You let it happen! You stood by watching while I had to kill two people!'

'Uh-huh?' I said. 'Yeah?'

'What the hell do you mean, "Uh-huh yeah"? Are you saying that you didn't do it, that it didn't happen that way? That you didn't plan the whole thing, an' – an'—'

'I ain't sayin' nothin' like that at all,' I said. 'All I'm saying or rather askin' is what you're goin' to tell folks. What kind of a believable explanation are you going to put together for them two dead bodies you got in your house and the blood all over the floor, and the fact that even an idjit could prove they was shot with your gun? Because no one's goin' to believe the truth, Rose; they just ain't goin' to believe no such wild story. You just think about it a minute, and you'll see that they won't.'

She opened her mouth to speak, to call me some more dirty names I guess. Then she seemed to have some second thoughts on the matter, and she sat down quietly at the side of the lounge.

'You've got to help me, Nick. You've got to help me cover this up some way.'

'Well, now, I don't rightly see how I could do that,' I said. 'After all, you're guilty of murder an' fornicatin' and hypocrisy, an'—'

'Huh! *Wha-at!*' She glared at me. 'Why, you fork-tongued son-of-a-bitch! You call me names after what you've done! And I don't suppose you're at all responsible, are you?'

'Not a speck,' I said. 'Just because I put temptation in front of people, it don't mean they got to pick it up.'

'I asked you a question, damn you! Who planned those murders? Who tells a lie every time he draws a breath? Who the hell is it that's been fornicating with me, and God knows how many others?'

'Oh, well,' I said. 'It don't count when I do those things.'

'It don't count! What the hell do you mean?'

I said I meant I was just doing my job, followin' the holy precepts laid down in the Bible. 'It's what I'm supposed to do, you know, to punish the heck out of people for bein' people. To coax 'em into revealin' theirselves, an' then kick the crap out of 'em. And it's a god-danged hard job, Rose, honey, and I figure that if I can get a little pleasure in the process of trappin' folks I'm mighty well entitled to it.'

Rose stared at me, frowning.

'What is this?' she said. 'What kind of nutty talk is that?'

'Well, now, I guess it does sound kind of nutty,' I said, 'but that ain't hardly no ways my fault. By rights, I should be rompin' on the high an' the mighty, the folks that really run this country. But I ain't allowed to touch them, so I've got to make up for it by being twice as hard on the white trash an' Negroes, and people like you that let their brains sink down to their butts because they couldn't find no place else to use them. Yes, sir, I'm laborin' in the Lord's vineyard, and if I can't reach up high, I got to work all the harder on the low-hangin' vines. For the Lord loveth a willin' worker, Rose; He liketh to see a man bustin' his ass during workin' hours. And I got them hours cut way, way down with eatin' and sleepin', but I can't eat and sleep all the time.'

I'd let my eyes drift shut while I was talking. When I opened them Rose was gone, but I heard her moving around in Myra's room.

I went to the door and looked in.

She'd stripped out of her clothes, and was trying on some of Myra's. I asked her if she was figurin' on going somewhere, and she gave me a look that would have fried an egg.

'Am I going somewhere,' she said bitterly. 'As if you didn't know what I was going to do, what I *have* to do!'

I said I reckoned she'd be taking the dawn train out of town, because no one would see her leave that way and she'd have a full day's start before I got excited and worried about Myra and Lennie and got around to discovering that they was murdered.

'Of course, that dawn train don't carry passengers, they just got a water-stop here. But I reckon them trainmen will be proud to let you ride when they see how friendly you are. I bet they won't charge you a cent, which makes things pretty nice since you don't have no money you can put your hands on.'

Rose bit her lips; shook her head wonderingly.

'You're actually enjoying this, aren't you? You're getting a kick out of it!'

'Not really,' I said. 'It's just part of my job, you know, to gloat over folks in trouble.'

'Nick,' she said. 'What's happened to you? When did you get like this?'

I said, well, sir, if she meant when had the truth been revealed to me, it had been happenin' for a long time. Bit by bit, I'd been given a glimpse of it, and now and then I'd think I knew what it was, and now an' then I was just mystified and scared. I didn't know from what for, and I'd get the idea that I must be goin' crazy or something. And then, tonight, at her house, as I stood outside of myself plannin' things, and then as I'd watched what I'd planned to take place, it was sort of like someone had pulled a trigger in my mind and there was one great big flash of light, and at last I saw the whole truth; at last I saw why things were as they were, and why I was as I was.

'I saw it all, honey,' I said. 'I saw the truth and the glory; and it ain't going to be nearways so bad for you as you might think. Why, a gal like you can make herself a mint in them river towns, just doin' what you like to do, and I never knew no gal that done it any better. And speakin' of that, and as long as we won't be seein' each other no more, I've got no objection to cleaving unto you for five or ten minutes even if you are sort of a fugitive from the law.'

Rose snatched up the alarm clock from the dresser and flang it at me. It smashed against the wall, and what I mean is it *really* smashed.

'Now, god-dang it, Rose,' I said. 'How the god-dang heck am I goin' to wake up in time for church?'

'Church! *Church!*' she moaned. 'You going to church after – after—! Oh, you son-of-a-bitch! Oh, you sneaky, tricky, lying, mealy-mouthed bastard!'

'Now, there you go again,' I said. 'There ain't no sure use of pretendin' no longer, 'cause now I *know* you're mad at me.'

She cut loose with another blast of cuss words. Then, she

whirled back around to the mirror, and began fussin' with the dress she was trying on.

'It's that Amy Mason, isn't it?' she said. 'You're getting rid of everyone so you can marry her.'

'Well,' I said. 'I got to admit I've been studyin' about it.'

'I'll bet you have! I just bet you have, you double-crossing skunk!'

'Yes, sir,' I said. 'I've been studyin' about it, but the fact is I can't make up my mind. It ain't that she's a sinner, because she's one of the quality an' they got their own laws and rules and I don't have to bother with 'em. But I'm afraid marryin' her might interfere with my work. Y'see, I got my job to do, Rose; I got to go on bein' High Sheriff, the highest legal authority in Potts County, this place that's the world to most people here, because they never see nothin' else. I just got to be High Sheriff, because I've been peccul-yarly an' singularly fitted for it, and I ain't allowed to give it up. Every now an' then, I think I'm goin' to get out of it, but always the thoughts are put in my head and the words in my mouth to hold me in my place. I got to be it, Rose. I got to be High Sheriff of Potts County forever an' ever. I got to go on an' on, doin' the Lord's work; and all he does is the pointin' Rose, all He does is pick out the people an' I got to exercise His wrath on 'em. And I'll tell you a secret, Rose, they's plenty of times when I don't agree with Him at all. But I got nothing to say about it. I'm the High Sheriff of Potts County, an' I ain't supposed to do nothing that really needs doing, nothin' that might jeopardize my job. All I can do is follow the pointin' of the Lord's finger, striking down the pore sinners that no one gives a good god-dang about. Like I say, I've tried to get out of it; I've figured on runnin' away and stayin' away. But I can't, and I know I'll never be able to. I got to keep on like I'm doin' now, and I'm afraid Amy would never understand that or put up with it. So I misdoubt I'll be marryin' her.'

Rose gazed at me in the mirror. She studied me for a long time, puzzled, angry, frightened, and then she shrugged and rolled her eyes.

'Oh, brother!' she said. 'What a bull artist!'

'Now, god-dang it, Rose,' I said. 'You just think about it a little and it'll make plenty of sense for you. Ain't it logical that I should appear here in Potts County, which is just about as close to the asshole of creation as you can get without havin' a finger snapped off? And don't I have to be just another fella – just a man, like I was the first time – and don't I have to act like one, just the same as anyone else? When in Potts County, do what the Potts County folks do, like the fella says. An' if you want to promote anyone to glory, why do it privately, because people want logical explanations for everything, particularly for the miracle of promotin' people to glory.'

Rose made a farting noise with her lips. 'Brother!' she said again. 'Are you ever full of crap!'

'Now, don't you say that, Rose,' I said. 'Please, please don't. I've been a long time figuring things out, and now I finally done it; I finally explained things to myself, and I had to explain 'em, Rose, or go crazy. An' even now, sometimes, I find a doubt or so creepin' in, and I can't stand it, I honest to God can't stand it. So, please, honey, please don't . . . don't . . .'

I turned and stumbled off to my bedroom.

I prayed mightily and pretty soon I got a grip on myself, and my doubts went away. I prayed mightily and the strength flowed back into me, and I didn't hardly mind at all the names that Rose was fussin' and cussin' at me. And I could even have kissed her goodbye when she left, and maybe've given her a pinch or two, if she hadn't threatened to brain me if I so much as touched her.

24

I went to church like always, and I was asked to sing in the choir like I'd been doin' up until the time it had looked like Sam Gaddis was going to beat me out for sheriff. So I sang out loud an' clear, shouting the praises of the Lord, and goddang if I didn't practically raise the roof with Amens when the minister started preachin'. I reckon I must've prayed and shouted an' sang louder than anyone in the church, and after everything was over the minister wrung me by the hand and called me Brother, and said he saw the spirit was truly in me.

'And where is good Sister Myra today? Not ill, I hope.'

'Well, no, I reckon not,' I said. 'She and Lennie drove out to see Sister Rose Hauck last night, and I didn't discover until this morning that the horse had run off and come back to town by hisself. I guess that's what happened, anyway, because the horse is in the stable an' she and Lennie ain't come home yet.'

'Yes?' He frowned a little. 'But haven't you phoned the Hauck house?'

'Oh, I didn't see no point in that,' I said. 'I couldn't have picked her up, anyway, before church and I sure didn't want to miss church. I figured I'll probably drive out in time to bring her in for evenin' services.'

'Yes,' he said, still kind of frowning. 'Well . . .'

'Hallelujah!' I said. 'Praise the Lord, Brother!'

I went on home, and fixed myself a bite to eat. Then I

washed up the dishes, and put 'em away, and after I'd done that I went into my room and dropped down on the bed. Just laid there, doin' nothing in particular and not workin' very hard at it.

I found a long hair sticking out of my nose, and I jerked it out and looked at it, and it didn't look particularly interesting. I dropped it to the floor, wonderin' if falling hair from fellas' noses was noted along with fallin' sparrows. I raised up on one cheek of my butt, and eased out one of those long rattly farts, like you never can get rid of when other folks are around. I scratched my balls, tryin' to decide at what point a fella stopped scratchin' and started playin'. Which is an age-old question, I guess, and one that ain't likely to be solved in the near future.

I listened, tryin' to hear Myra out in the kitchen. I started puzzlin' over where Lennie might be, and thinking maybe I ought to go out and look for him before he got into trouble. I wondered if maybe I shouldn't take a run out to see Rose, and pleasure her up a little if Tom wasn't to home.

It seemed like a good idea, the more I thought about it. And I was clean out into the living room before I suddenly remembered; and I dropped down hard into a chair, and buried my face in my hands. Trying to sort things out. Trying to fit them back together in the only way they made sense.

Buck came in – Ken Lacey's deputy, you know. I was kind of befuddled for a minute, so absorbed with fittin' things together that I couldn't quite place him. But there was the gun hangin' from his hip and his deputy sheriff's badge and his long leathery face, so of course I remembered pretty fast.

We shook hands and I told him to set down. 'I bet you prob'ly run into my wife downtown,' I said. 'I bet she told you just to come right on up here and walk in without knockin', because I wouldn't mind a bit, didn't she?'

'Nope,' said Buck.

'You mean it didn't happen that way?'

'Yep,' said Buck.

'Yeah?'

'Yeah,' said Buck. 'What happened was I was huntin' me a skunk, and when I'm a-huntin' skunk I don't stand none on ceremony, I just bust right in wherever I smell him.'

'Well,' I said. 'Well, now. How you standin' all this weather?'

'Tol'able. Just tol'able.'

'You reckon it's goin' to get any hotter?'

'Yep,' said Buck. 'Yes, sir, it's goin' to get a lot hotter. Wouldn't suprise me none if it got so hot for a certain fella that didn't keep his bounden bargain with me that he just naturally won't be able to stand it.'

I got a bottle out of the sideboard and filled a couple of glasses. He took the one I handed him, and threw it against the wall.

'Like to keep my hands free,' he explained. 'Kind of a habit with me when I'm around a fella that don't keep his bounden agreements.'

'Buck,' I said. 'I just couldn't do it! I was willin' to but it was just plumb impossible!'

'No, it wasn't,' Buck said. 'Moresomeover, it ain't.'

'But you don't understand, god-dang it! I possolutely couldn't do it because—'

'Ain't interested in no becauses or whys or whichfors,' Buck said. 'You 'n' me had a bargain, and I done my part in gettin' Ken down here. Now you do your part an' drop that rope over his neck, or I'm goin' to put it around yours.'

I told him that would be a pretty trick to see, but maybe he'd better not attempt it. 'Might be you'd get it around your own neck.'

'Maybe,' Buck said. 'But then I reckon not. I reckon I could go right on a-playin' a part, like I got so much practice doin' around Ken Lacey.'

'Such as?' I said.

'Such as bein' in such a state of fear and tremblin' that I didn't dast do anything when you told me you was goin' to kill them two pimps. Also, along with being feared and trembly, I was just plain stupid, and I didn't reckon there was no way we could ever convict you until this fella, George Barnes, came along and he don't like you none at all nohow an' I figure he could somehow prove the truth with me tellin' him what it was, an' also swearin' to it.'

'Buck,' I said. 'Listen to me, Buck . . .'

'Uh-huh.' Buck shook his head. 'I et a peck of dirt a day, every day I worked for Ken Lacey. Et so much dirt that I could feel it seepint out of me, and I couldn't hardly bear to hug my kids no more nor t'sleep with my wife for fear it would rub off on them, and they couldn't never get clean like I figured I couldn't never get clean. Well, now, I got a chance to stop eatin' it and put Ken Lacey under six feet of it. And don't you try to stop me, Nick. You try to stop me, and t'me you're just Ken Lacey; you're his twin brother, spoonin' the dirt into me every time I open my mouth, and I just can't eat no more. I just can't, by God, I CAN'T EAT NO MORE DIRT! I C-CAN'T—'

His jaw snapped shut. He brushed his nose with his sleeve, his eyes burnin' into mine. 'That's it, Nick. I'd rather it was Ken, but it's goin' to be you or him.'

I took a drink from my glass, giving him time to get calmed down a little.

Then I told him why he couldn't do it, revealin' who I was for the first time. He didn't seem a speck surprised, beyond raising his eyebrows for a second. The fact was, I guess, that he probably thought I was jokin' or crazy – he didn't care much which. An' I suppose I should have expected that – because what would you have thought? – but I was still a mite disappointed.

I told him again, just to make sure he'd heard me right. He shook his head, sayin' he reckoned I was wrong.

'Prob'ly got yourself mixed up with that other fella,' he said. 'The one with the same front initial.'

'That's right, Buck!' I said. 'That's right! I'm both, don't you see? The fella that gets betrayed and the one that does the betrayin' all in one man!'

He didn't seem even nowheres near convinced. I jumped up and went over to the window, thinkin' that maybe I would see a sign. But all I could see was a couple of dogs, frolickin' around and sniffing each other.

I stood watching them, and I guess I laughed out loud without knowin' it.

'That grave-dirt ticklin' you?' Buck drawled. 'You already got one foot in it, you know.'

'I was just watching a couple of dogs out here,' I said, 'and it reminded me of a story I heard one time. You ever hear it, Buck? – I mean why dogs always go around sniffing each other's asses?'

Buck said he hadn't heard it. 'Can't say that I'm real interested in hearin' it, neither, just in case you was figurin' on telling it.'

I said, that, well, sir, accordin' to this story, all the dogs in the world held a convention back in the beginning of time, their purpose being to set up a code of conduct, like maybe it shouldn't be fair to bite each other in the balls and so on. And there was this one dog that had a copy of Robert's Rules of Order that he'd got somewhere, prob'ly at the same place Cain got his wife. So he automatically became chairman, and the first thing he done was to declare the entire convention a committee of the hole. 'Fellas,' he says, 'canines of the convention. I don't want to tread on no honorable dogs' paws, so I'll just put it this way. When we go back in them smoke-filled rooms to caucus, I'm sure we don't want to smell nothing but smoke, and the best thing to do it seems to me is to pile our assholes outside, and if someone will make a motion to that effect, I'll certainly be glad to put a second on it.' Well, sir, it seemed like such a danged good idea that every dog in the convention jumped up to make the motion, so the chairman declared it passed by acclamation, and there was a brief recess while all the dogs went outside to stack up their assholes. Then, they went back inside t'carry out their business. And god-danged if a heck of a storm didn't blow up out of nowhere, and it scattered them assholes every which way, mixin' 'em up so bad that not a one of them dogs was ever able to find his own. So that's why they still go around sniffing butts, and they'll probably keep on until the end of time. Because a dog that's lost his ass just can't be happy, even if one of 'em is pretty much like another, and the one he has is in good working order.

'What I'm saying is this, Buck,' I said. 'Hang on to your own ass, and don't try to get Ken's. For all you know, he may be eatin' a lot worse than dirt and I may be too, and you'll be a lot happier like you are.'

'Is that all you got to say?' Buck said, and I could hear him getting up from his chair. 'You're sure that's all you got to say?'

I hesitated, thinkin' I should be able to come up with somethin'. Because it was all so clear to me, Christ knew it was clear: love one another and don't screw no one unless they're bending over, and forgive us our trespasses because we may be a minority of one. For God's sake, *for God's sake* – why else had I been put here in Potts County, and why else did I stay here? Why else, who else, what else but Christ Almighty would put up with it?

But I couldn't make him see that. He was as blind as the rest of 'em.

'Well, Nick? I ain't waiting much longer.'

'And you don't have to, Buck,' I said. 'You don't have to because I finally come to a decision. I've been a long time comin' to it; it's been the product of thinkin' and thinkin' and thinkin', and then some more thinkin'. And dependin' on how you look at it, it's the god-dangest whingdingest decision ever made, or it's the skitty-assed worst. Because it explains everything that goes on in the world – it answers everything and it answers nothing.

'So here it is, Buck, here's my decision. I thought and I thought and then I thought some more, and finally I came to a decision. I decided I don't no more know what to do than if I was just another lousy human being!'